HUNGER

JACKIE MORSE KESSLER

Houghton Mifflin Harcourt

Boston New York 2010

IF YOU HAVE EVER LOOKED IN THE MIRROR

AND HATED WHAT YOU SAW, THIS BOOK

IS FOR YOU.

For information about permission to
reproduce selections from this book, write to
Permissions
Houghton Mifflin Harcourt Publishing Company
215 Park Avenue South, New York, New York 10003

Graphia and the Graphia logo are registered trademarks of
Houghton Mifflin Harcourt Publishing Company.

www.hmhbooks.com

The text of this book is set in Adobe Garamond.
Book design by Susanna Vagt.

Library of Congress Cataloging-in-Publication Data
Kessler, Jackie Morse.
Hunger / Jackie Morse Kessler.
p. cm.
Summary: Seventeen-year-old Lisabeth has anorexia, and even turning into
Famine—one of the Four Horsemen of the Apocalypse—cannot keep her
from feeling fat and worthless.
ISBN 978-0-547-34124-8 (pbk. original : alk. paper) [1. Anorexia
nervosa--Fiction. 2. Eating disorders—Fiction. 3. Emotional
problems—Fiction. 4. Four Horsemen of the Apocalypse—Fiction.]
I. Title.
PZ7.K4835Hu 2010
[Fic]—dc22
2009050009

Manufactured in the United States of America
DOM 10 9 8 7 6 5 4 3 2 1
4500251676

Chapter 1

Lisabeth Lewis didn't mean to become Famine. She had a love affair with food, and she'd never liked horses (never mind the time she asked for a pony when she was eight; that was just a girl thing). If she'd been asked which Horseman of the Apocalypse she would most likely be, she would have probably replied, "War." And if you'd heard her and her boyfriend, James, fighting, you would have agreed. Lisa wasn't a Famine person, despite the eating disorder.

And yet there she was, Lisabeth Lewis, seventeen and no longer thinking about killing herself, holding the Scales of office. Famine, apparently, had scales—an old-fashioned balancing device made of brass or bronze or some other metal. What she was supposed to do with the Scales, she had no idea. Then again, the whole "Thou art the Black Rider; go thee out unto the world" thing hadn't really sunk in yet.

Alone in her bedroom, Lisa sat on her canopied bed with its overflowing pink and white ruffles, and she stared at the metal balance, wondering what, exactly, she'd promised the pale man in the messenger's uniform. Or had it been a robe? Frowning, she tried to picture the delivery man who'd just left—but the more she grasped for it, the more slippery his image became until Lisa was left with the impression of a person painted in careless watercolors.

Maybe the Lexapro was messing with her.

Yeah, she thought, putting the Scales on her nightstand, next to a half-empty glass of water (which rested on a coaster) and a pile of white pills (which did not), *I'm high as a freaking kite.*

And you're fat, lamented the negative voice, the Thin voice, Lisa's best friend and worst critic, the one that whispered to her in her sleep and haunted her when she was awake.

High and fat, Lisa amended. *But at least I'm not depressed.*

Or dead; the delivery man had rung the doorbell before Lisa could swallow more than three of her mother's antidepressants. Bundled in her white terry cloth bathrobe over her baggy flannel pajamas, Lisa had answered the door and accepted the parcel.

"For thee," the pale man had said. "Thou art Famine."

And once Lisa had opened the oddly shaped package, all thoughts of suicide had drifted away. Thanks to the pills, that was sort of the way she was feeling now, as if she were drifting—drifting slowly like a cloud in the summertime sky, a cloud shaped like a set of old-fashioned scales . . .

The pills.

Pulling her gaze from the Scales, Lisa scooped the pills into her nightstand drawer. She wiped away the stray trails of powder, brushed off her hands, and gently closed the drawer. It wasn't as if she had to worry whether her mom would notice that her stash of bliss had been depleted; Mrs. Simon Lewis was off at some charity event or another, accepting some award or another. Lisa just didn't want to leave a mess. Even if she *had* overdosed, as she had originally planned, she would have died neatly in her own bed. Lisa tried her best to be considerate.

She frowned at the Scales. Dappled in moonlight there on her nightstand, they gleamed enticingly. Lisa couldn't decide if they looked ominous or merely cheesy.

Cheddar cheese, one ounce, the Thin voice announced. *One hundred fourteen point three calories. Nine point four grams of fat. Forty minutes on the exercise bike.*

And behind that, the pale man's words burned in Lisa's mind: *"Thou art Famine."*

Uh-huh. Right.

Famine having a set of old-fashioned scales, Lisa decided, was stupid. The only scales that mattered were the digital sort, the ones that also displayed your body mass index.

Lisa yawned. Her head was fuzzy, and everything seemed pleasantly blurred, soft around the edges. It was peaceful. She thought about closing her window shade, but she decided she liked the moonlight shining on the Scales—sort of a celestial spotlight.

You're loopy, she scolded herself. *Hallucinating. Get some sleep, Lisa.*

She settled down on her bed, pulling the princess pink covers around her to fend off the chill. Lately, she was always cold—and hungry. Although she enjoyed the feeling of hunger, she hated it when her body shivered. Whenever she forced her body to stop shivering, it made her teeth chatter. And when she forced her teeth to clamp shut, her body shivered. It was a physical conspiracy.

Lisa gripped the blankets tightly and started thinking about the homemade cookies she'd make for Tammy tomorrow. As she imagined the smell of chocolate chips, she calmed down.

Baking was soothing. And Tammy was a fiend for Lisa's baking. James was, too, but he always acted hurt when she wouldn't taste any of the sweets she made for him.

Snuggled like a baby, Lisa stared at the object on her nightstand. Backlit by the moon, the Scales seemed to wink at her.

"Thou art Famine."

She let out a bemused laugh. Famine. Really. She would have made a much better War.

Smiling, Lisa closed her eyes.

|||||

The black horse was in the garden directly beneath Lisa's window, invisible, waiting for its mistress to climb atop its back and go places she had never imagined—the smoke-filled dance clubs of Lagos, dripping with wealth and hedonism; the opulent world of Monte Carlo, oozing with indulgence; the streets of New Orleans, filled with its dizzying smells and succulent foods. In particular, the horse had a fondness for Nola's sweet pralines.

Perhaps they would go to Louisiana first—perhaps even tonight.

The black horse snorted and pawed the grass, chiding itself in the way that horses do. So what that it wished to move, to fly, to soar across the world and feast? It was a good steed; it would wait forever, if needed, until its mistress was ready to ride.

It wasn't the horse's fault that it was impatient; the rhododendrons in the garden couldn't mask the cloying odor of rot, which made the horse's large nostrils flare. Death had come and gone, but its scent had left its impression on the land, in the air.

Death was scary. The horse much preferred the smell of sugar. Or pralines.

The black horse waited, and Lisabeth Lewis, the new incarnation of Famine, dreamed of fields of dust.

CHAPTER 2

"Famine?" Tammy said, reaching for another cookie. "Like the disease?"

"Is it a disease? I thought it's a condition," Lisa said, putting a third pan into the oven. The kitchen was heavy with the aroma of freshly baked cookies, and Lisa's growling stomach was currently duking it out with her salivary glands to see which part of her body would be more embarrassing. She was practically foaming at the mouth as she imagined the taste of a cookie crumb nestled on her tongue, evaporating slowly as her saliva broke the bit down—but then a particularly loud whine from her middle region ruined the daydream and put the contest in the tank for her belly.

Stupid body. She slammed the oven door shut and mopped a mitted hand over her brow. The blast of oven heat, though brief, had been blissful. God, she felt like she'd never be warm again. Even her turtleneck sweater wasn't enough to block away the chill.

"Pregnancy is a condition," Tammy said after she finished her cookie. "Famine's a disease."

"So wouldn't that make it Pestilence?"

"No, that's like for bugs. You know, West Nile virus, black plague fleas, swine flu."

"Pigs aren't bugs."

"Same thing," Tammy insisted. "Pestilence is animals. Famine is people. It's a disease."

Lisa didn't want to argue, not with Tammy. She never argued with Tammy. She pulled off her oven mitts and set them on the counter, next to the mixing bowl still a quarter full of batter. "Whatever. But yeah, I was Famine. I had these scales, too. You know, the old-fashioned ones, like you see in legal seals and things."

"Cool."

"I guess." When Lisa had woken up late that morning, she'd looked at her nightstand, convinced she'd see a bronze balance perched there. But no; there had only been her mostly empty water glass and her small alarm clock.

"It is. It's ironic." Tammy was in Lisa's English lit class, where they were studying parody and satire, so she spoke from authority. "You've got a sense of humor when you dream."

"What do you mean?"

"You, as Famine. It's funny. I'm getting more milk."

"It's stupid, is what it is," Lisa said, spooning out more cookie dough onto a baking sheet. She'd made too much, even for Tammy's appetite; she'd have to give some to James later, and a few to her father. Maybe she'd even leave some for her mom for when she returned tomorrow night—or not. "It's not like I don't care about other people, or global hunger, or anything like that. I care." She was, in fact, in three social awareness groups in school. Granted, her mother had strong-armed her into joining to beef up her college applications, and Lisa was a member of those groups in name only. But it still proved that she cared—at least, on paper.

"Of course you do," Tammy said, pouring a second glass of milk. "You're one of the most sensitive people I know."

"So why would I come up with Famine?"

"Like I said, your subconscious has a sense of humor. I mean, Famine? You? You never eat junk food. You exercise every day."

She did. Multiple times per day. Lisa stood a little straighter as she slapped raw dough onto the cookie tray.

"That's not Famine," Tammy continued. "That's like the opposite of Famine. You're healthy."

Unbidden, Lisa remembered the last words Suzanne had said to her—Suzanne, her so-called best friend, her one-time childhood pal. Last week, Suzanne hadn't said Lisa was healthy. No, Suzanne had called her a name, basically telling her she was a mental case.

"You need help," Suzanne tells her.

"I don't!"

"You're sick, Leese. Don't you see that?"

"You're crazy!" Lisa clamps her hands over her ears, but that doesn't stop her from hearing the last thing Suzanne has to say, the words shaky and broken with tears:

"You're anorexic, Lisa."

Lisa pressed her lips together, surprised by a rush of anger as foreign as it was brief. The feeling ebbed, vanished, leaving behind a dull ache, a pang of loss. She had food issues. She knew that. But she wasn't anorexic. That was ridiculous.

You're not skinny enough to be anorexic, the Thin voice whispered. *If you were anorexic, your belly wouldn't still pook out over the top of your jeans.*

Lisa imagined her fingers tracing over the curve of her abdomen, made all the more prominent by the low-rise jeans she wore. And yes, her lower belly did still pook out.

Anorexics don't have muffin tops, the Thin voice said. *You're not anorexic. You're just fat.*

And she was. No matter how much weight she lost, Lisa would always be fat. She just knew it. She also knew the thought should make her feel sad, or mad, or . . . well, *something.* But she didn't feel anything inside, except maybe scooped out. Hollow.

Lisa grimaced, concentrating on scraping the last of the dough from the sides of the glass mixing bowl. Suzanne was insane. Jealous. She wasn't a real friend, not like Tammy.

"If my subconscious was trying to twist things around," Lisa said, "wouldn't it focus on how fat I was? It wouldn't be about taking food away from other people." The very notion made Lisa shudder. "Me being Famine is just dumb."

"It was a *dream,* Leese. What's the big deal?"

Lisa floundered, trying to properly frame her outrage. "Famine hurts lots of people. Famine's a bad guy."

"So? Some part of you sees yourself as a bad guy."

"Apocalyptically bad? That's crazy." Right. She was just suicidally bad.

Tammy shrugged, taking her last cookie from the plate. Lisa knew it would be the last one; Tammy ate twenty cookies, like clockwork, unless she also spread frosting on them. Then she maxed out at twelve. Lisa knew; she counted things. "Part of you thinks so," Tammy said around her mouthful of chocolate-chip sweetness. "That's the Columbine in you."

Lisa glanced at her friend. "The what?"

"The deep down, angsty part of you that wants to take your rage out on the world at large," Tammy said, obnoxiously chipper. "Your own personal Columbine. That's what your Famine is. Your subconscious just wrapped the rage up in a food image, instead of a freak-with-a-gun image. You relate better to food, that's all."

Troubled, Lisa put the empty mixing bowl and spoon into the sink, squirted in some liquid soap, and ran the hot water. Watching the bowl soak, she thought about Tammy's words. She knew she had rage inside of her—real rage, not the momentary flare-ups she had whenever James or her mother got under her skin. Yes, that anger was inside of her . . . somewhere. Lately, it was hard for Lisa to feel much of anything.

No, she could feel, all right. She felt fat—and so empty inside. That emptiness echoed through her even now, chilling her, leaving its damp and dank impression upon her skin, upon her soul.

A soap bubble drifted up, joyous, glistening in the afternoon light cast through the window by the sink. Lisa watched it dance in the air as she heard Tammy chug down the last of the milk, and she blinked when the bubble popped into nothingness. She didn't realize she was crying until a tear hovered by the corner of her mouth. Her tongue poked out, lapping at it greedily; salty sweetness, pure, calorie free.

"Back in about twenty," Tammy said, scraping her chair on the wooden floor.

Pulled out of her pensive reflection of loneliness, Lisa said, "Use the bathroom upstairs. The one down here's getting clogged easily. Grab the Lysol, though."

"Yes, Mom."

Off Tammy went to take care of her afternoon snack, and Lisa set to cleaning the mixing bowl. Even after eight months of knowing Tammy, Lisa still held the girl in awe. Where Lisa was high strung, Tammy was casual. When Lisa worried, Tammy laughed. She exuded self-confidence—a sort of power—that Lisa would never possess.

As with food. Lisa could never get herself to bring anything up. The one time she'd tried, she'd felt as if she were choking. Her fingers had squirmed there in her throat like sausages jumping on a hot skillet, and she'd chickened out before she could do more than cough up the first gut-wrenching spray of bile. She'd scrubbed her hand ten times and gargled with Listerine for two minutes. She hadn't told Tammy about her colossal failure. How could she? Tammy was disciplined when it came to food. She could bring up a doughnut in thirty seconds. Not that Lisa had ever seen it, let alone timed it. But Tammy had told her so, proudly, back when they were first sharing their secrets all those months ago.

Yes, Tammy was disciplined—not like Lisa. For Lisa, it was a constant struggle.

She scoured the mixing bowl until her fingers pruned. She turned off the water and placed the mixing bowl and wooden spoon in the drying rack. Maybe one day, she would be able to control her body the way Tammy controlled hers.

Maybe. She hoped.

The timer dinged, and Lisa pulled out the cookies from the oven and placed the baking sheet on the stovetop to cool for a minute as she put the final pan in. She hummed, softly and out of key, as she slid the hot cookies off the baking sheet and onto the cooling rack on the counter. She couldn't have told you what she was humming, and because of how mournful it sounded, you probably wouldn't have recognized it.

Gingerly placing cookies onto the rack, Lisabeth continued humming a broken and bleeding version of the "Sesame Street" song that almost, but not quite, masked the sounds of Tammy retching upstairs.

‖‖‖‖

"Hey, Princess. Hi, Tammy."

"Hi, Daddy," Lisa said, giving Simon Lewis a welcome-home peck on the cheek. He had a balding head, a trim beard, and kind eyes. Not too tall, not too short, he was incredibly average, from his build to his clothing. Lisa thought he was perfect.

"Hi, Mr. Lewis." Sitting at the breakfast nook, shuffling a deck of cards, Tammy gave him a carefree wave. "Lisa baked cookies. There's plenty."

"I can see that," he said with a laugh. To Lisa he added, "You know your mother would read me the riot act if she caught me sneaking a cookie."

"It's not sneaking," Lisa said, offering a plate of cookies. "I'm giving them to you."

Her father relented and took two. "I have to finish up some paperwork, so I'll be upstairs. I was thinking Chinese for dinner. Sound good, Princess?"

"Sure," Lisa said.

The Thin voice whispered, *Brown rice, one hundred thirty-five calories. Steamed broccoli, two cups, fifty calories. One bite of chicken, thirty-six calories. Two hours on the exercise bike.*

She'd have to put in extra time during her evening workout, but that was doable. Besides, she liked opening the fortune cookies.

He looked at Tammy. "You'll stay for dinner, of course?"

"Wish I could," Tammy said, sounding sad. "But I promised my mom I'd be home for dinner."

That was an utter lie; Tammy's mother was away for the weekend. But Lisa didn't call her on it. While Tammy had no compunction about eating in front of Lisa, she didn't like to eat around other people. It made Lisa feel privileged to be one of Tammy's trusted confidantes.

"Next time, then," Mr. Lewis said.

"You bet, sir."

Lisa's dad went off to do his paperwork, and the girls shared a he's-a-sweetie look. Tammy had told Lisa months ago that she preferred Mr. Lewis over her own father. "Your dad's cool," she had said back then. "He's smart and funny and charming, and he actually listens to what you tell him. Bet he doesn't get all absorbed in whatever sport's on TV, or red-faced about the morons in the office."

"My dad's perfect," Lisa had replied. Perfection, though, could be incredibly tough to emulate, let alone please. But Lisa kept trying. One day, she'd make her father proud. Her mother, on the other hand . . .

Lisa's stomach roiled, bringing with it a hint of anger. No, she wasn't going to waste time thinking about her mother; she had better things to do.

She sat on the stool opposite Tammy as her friend started to deal out the cards. Cutthroat spades. Good times. Lisa said, "Your mom's cooking, huh?"

Tammy actually looked chagrined. She shrugged, her smile sheepish. "Yeah, well. I love Chinese food. I'm not about to pig out in front of your dad. He'd lose his impression of me being all ladylike."

"I swear, you have a crush on my dad."

"Ew, gross."

"You are so Nabokov."

"As if. I bet his back's hairy," Tammy said, her eyes sparkling. "I don't mess around with guys who have back hair. But I bet your dad is a good kisser."

"La la la," Lisa said, covering her ears, "I can't hear you . . ."

Tammy finished her water. "Besides, he's happily married. I'm not into married guys."

"With back hair," Lisa said, thinking about her mom and dad and wondering, not for the first time, if her parents were, in fact, happily married. Her mother was supercharged and always running from one place to another—like this weekend. Which fundraising effort was she attending this time? Breast cancer research, supporting the troops, feeding the hungry . . . After a while, it all blurred. There was always a cause for her mother to rally behind. And the cause was always far from home. Her dad, by contrast, was more of a slow, steady person, a homebody. Dependable. Mom was the sports car; Dad was the all-terrain vehicle.

It doesn't matter, Lisa told herself. Either her parents were happy together or they weren't. Lisa didn't want to think about it anymore. Instead, she focused on playing cards.

In a little while, Lisa's dad came back into the kitchen and got Lisa's dinner choice (H4 on the takeout menu: steamed chicken and broccoli, brown rice), called in their dinner order, and gave his daughter a kiss as he left to pick up the food.

"He's cool," Tammy said.

"Yeah."

"Just not in a doable way."

"Oh God." Lisa, appalled, tried to scrub away the image of her father and her friend going at it like rabbits. "I'm going to have nightmares now." Right up there with her being Famine.

"Happy to contribute to your therapist's bills. Anyway, I'm off." Tammy slid down from her stool and grabbed her leather jacket from where it hung over a kitchen chair. "You coming over tomorrow?"

"One o'clock," Lisa said, agreeing to their usual Sunday time. "I'll bring cookies."

"You're a goddess." Tammy waved and opened the back door to let herself out. Lisa got up from her stool to see her friend off.

It was already bordering on darkness outside; evening came earlier and earlier with every passing day. But even with the dim light and Tammy partially blocking her view, Lisa saw the horse. It stood there in the garden, black as burned toast and tall as anything. It looked directly at her, its white eyes glowing, steam blowing from its nostrils.

Lisa let out a startled gasp.

"What? What is it?" Tammy looked out, obviously trying to see what had made Lisa react as if she'd seen a ghost. "Leese?"

"There, in the garden! The horse!" Lisa pointed, her hand shaking.

Tammy now stood completely in the doorway, blocking Lisa's view. Hands on her hips, she looked out, her posture defiant. After a moment, she said, "There's nothing out here, Leese."

Lisa nudged her way in front of Tammy—and stared directly at the horse.

"Your eyes are playing tricks on you," Tammy said.

Her voice small, Lisa said, "You don't see it?"

"Wish I did. A horse, here in your backyard? How cool would that be?"

Staring at the black horse, Lisa didn't think it was cool at all.

The horse cocked its head, then dug its hoof into the soil. Clearly, it was impatient. Based on how it was glaring at Lisa with those creepy white eyes, it was impatient with *her*.

"Sorry," Tammy said, "no horse here. I'll see you tomorrow. Tell James I said hi."

With that, Tammy walked out of the doorway, sauntering directly past the black horse. As if they'd previously agreed to terms, both the girl and the horse ignored each other; Tammy walked quickly in the cold evening, and the horse stared at Lisa.

Her breath caught in her throat, and Lisa realized she was about to scream, so she slammed the door and leaned against it, breathing too fast. She was sweating now. *Seeing things,* she told herself. *Just seeing things.*

Calming herself, she looked up. And she saw the Scales of Famine on the kitchen table.

This time, Lisa screamed long and loud.

CHAPTER 3

Her voice gave out, and her mouth gaped as she stared at the set of scales on the table.

Oh God, it's real, it's real, it's real.

She stared at the metal balance, its plates gleaming, beckoning. If not for her nightmare, she might have guessed that the object was just an eccentric centerpiece.

For an unknown amount of time, Lisa balanced on the precipice of madness. Her world consisted of the Scales in front of her, and the threat of the horse outside, and herself, cowering by the back door. She remembered the delivery man from her dream, her nightmare, with his cold voice and colder words.

"For thee. Thou art Famine."

No, she thought frantically, her heartbeat a climbing gallop.

"Thou art the Black Rider."

Now her chest hitched, and she couldn't take a proper breath. *Please, no.*

"Go thee out unto the world."

Lisa tried to laugh, tried to scream again, but her throat constricted and her protest died on her tongue. *I'm losing my mind,* she thought. And she was right.

But then the Thin voice saved her.

Hershey's Kisses, it whispered. *Twenty-five calories each.*

Lisa took a shaky breath.

Hostess CupCakes, one hundred eighty-one calories, six grams of fat.

Lisa exhaled, slowly, and found that she could think again.

The old-fashioned balance stood on the kitchen table, mocking her with its very presence. Its plates reflected the overhead light, sparkling like metallic laughter.

It was laughing at her.

Part of her flinched, wanting to run to her bedroom. But a quiet part of her—the part where the Thin voice lived, perhaps—resented being made to retreat inside the safety of her home. Though the refrigerator magnet said SANDY'S KITCHEN, Lisabeth knew, felt, that the kitchen was actually her own. This was where she made coffee for her dad every morning. This was where she carefully packaged a lunch that she brought to school, stuffed with negative foods such as rice cakes and celery. This was where she chopped and sautéed and sliced and mixed and baked. This was the place where she exerted control—if not necessarily over her body, then over the foods she prepared for herself and for others.

No one made Lisa shrink away from her kitchen.

Strengthened, Lisa took a step forward. Then another. And then she strode over to the table and reached out to touch the Scales.

The back door opened, and her father called out, "Soup's on!"

Lisa whirled around, startled.

"Hey," her father said as he deposited an overstuffed brown bag on the counter. "What's that I see?"

Lisa looked at the table, an odd mix of guilt and anticipation rising in her chest. She said nothing as she waited for her
father to pronounce her sane by confirming the presence of the
Scales.

"You didn't set the table."

Lisa's mouth opened, then closed. She glanced over her
shoulder at her father, who was looking right at the table. If he
noticed the large balance smack dab in the center, he chose to
keep the revelation to himself.

"Princess," her father said, his voice gentle, yet still full of
reproach. "What happened? Did you get too caught up in your
card game?"

"Sorry, Daddy." Her voice was raw, harsh to her ears. "I got
distracted."

"Whatever could distract my seventeen-year-old daughter
on a Saturday evening? Certainly not the thought of her boyfriend picking her up in two hours." Her father let out a wry
chuckle. "Daydream about James later, Princess. Please set the
table."

Blushing, Lisa took plates out of the cabinet, grabbed two
cloth napkins, and rummaged in the silverware drawer. Her
gaze locked on the Scales, she set the table for two, careful not
to touch the balance with the plates.

Mr. Lewis approached, plastic containers in his hands. Lisa
stepped aside.

He has to see it, she thought. *There's no room for the food and
the plates and the—*

For a moment, her father blocked her view. Then he straightened up as he stepped away, and Lisa saw that where the Scales

had been, now there was a container of steamed chicken and broccoli, a carton of steamed brown rice, and a smaller carton of roast pork fried rice.

Lisa bolted to the back door and wrenched it open. In the darkness of night, the horse's eyes glowed like twin stars.

Her blood pounded in her ears, thunderous, each beat pronouncing doom. She felt as if she were going to faint.

"Princess? What's wrong?" Lisa heard her father come stand behind her. "What is it?" he asked, sounding concerned.

The horse let out a snort, as if it, too, were gently reproaching her.

"Nothing," she said quietly, staring at the dark horse in the open darkness of the garden, black on black. "It's nothing."

⦚⦚⦚

In the garden, the horse chuffed out another breath. Although it wanted to roam once again—feel its hooves trod upon impressionable soil as its mane and tail danced in the wind, taste the delights the world had to offer—its rider was not yet ready.

The horse's ears flicked back, in a sort of equine shrug. It didn't mind waiting in the garden, not really. After all the places it had traveled recently, it didn't mind a short break.

It regarded the rhododendrons, greens giving way to scarlets as autumn advanced, and it let out a sigh. Pretty, certainly. But not as good as pralines.

The horse might have been amused if it had known about the human saying, "If wishes were horses, dreamers would ride." Its rider was not the dreamer of the Four. That description belonged to Death. Even so, the horse wished it had something sweet upon its tongue.

Soon, soon. When a creature lived forever, waiting was as second nature as breathing.

Thinking about the foods to come, the horse bent its head to the bush and began to nibble.

Inside the Lewis house, Lisabeth chewed and chewed and chewed her food. As she swallowed, around the world, hunger was momentarily sated.

████

James was fifteen minutes late, as usual. Normally, Lisa wasn't bothered by his habitual tardiness. Tonight, though, her temper was short, and she welcomed him with an acerbic tongue barely softened by her chaste kiss on his cheek. "Watch broken again?"

"Cut my head off much?" he replied, an easy smile on his face. Clearly, he wasn't rising to the bait—not yet, anyway.

She relented. "I'm a bit tense," she said by way of apology. James had come via the front door. No black horse loitering by the mailbox, at least; she'd checked—twice.

"I can see that." Standing in the doorway, he peered at her, his gaze intense, drinking in her features until she wanted to beg him to look away. "You look tired," he said.

She nodded. "Didn't sleep well last night." That was the God's honest truth.

"Sorry," he said, sheepish. He reached for her hand and held it firmly. His was large and deliciously warm around hers. "I know at least part of that's my fault."

She didn't deny it; their fight last night had been spectacular. Lisa didn't even remember what it had been about; she had a hard time recalling details lately. Specifics seemed to blur, smeared memories in her mind like oil stains. Take last night's fight: here, a smudge of James's words, hesitant like his fingers tracing the curve of her waist; there, a blot of her accusations, ugly as the cellulite on her thighs. Their voices raised, all reds and blacks, overripe and rotting. Try as she might, the heated argument last night was nothing clearer than that: impressions of feelings, emphasized with color.

He had apologized, though—that much she did remember. His hands, caressing her face, gently brushing away her tears. His lips, pressing against hers so softly, as if afraid she would bruise. A tender "I'm so sorry," and her chest fluttered, loosened. She could still taste the ghost of him on her lips even now: mint gum and a hint of apple.

Surely she'd remember something that had left her so depressed that she'd attempted to kill herself by overdosing. But she didn't. Maybe she could have recalled the fight, if she tried hard enough—there had been a time not so long ago when she was able to remember details of their arguments down to the smug looks and angry gestures. But now she just didn't have the energy.

Lisa smiled at James. It felt tight on her face. "It's okay," she said, not exactly lying.

"If you're not up for it, we don't have to go out. We can stay in, watch something on HBO," he said, then added with a wink, "Do that cuddling thing you girls like so much."

God, staying in sounded so nice. But she knew he wanted to go out. It had been, what, weeks since they'd actually done anything besides hang out at either his house or hers. "No, really. I'm fine. I'll just get my jacket."

He eyed her sweater. "You might not need it."

"You know me," she said lightly. "Always cold."

A long pause, then he said, "Cold hands, warm heart." He smiled at her, but his smile looked as strained as hers felt.

Flustered, she marched to the closet and yanked her jacket off its hanger. Was he still mad at her? Why was he getting weird about her wanting a coat? It wasn't as if it was the middle of summer. Nights were chilly. Everyone knew that. She'd even seen some people wearing gloves lately. Like the delivery man last night . . .

Lisa frowned. What had happened to the scales?

From upstairs, Mr. Lewis called out, "Is that James I hear?"

"Hello, sir," James said loudly.

Lisa's dad walked down the stairs, approaching the young couple. "Have you come to steal my daughter away?"

"Just for a few hours, sir."

"What are your intentions toward my daughter?"

James grinned, used to the ritual. Lisa, who never liked being discussed as if she were neither present nor an actual person, quietly slipped on her jacket. James announced, "To take her to a movie and bring her home before curfew."

"And what happens if you bring her home after curfew?"

James replied solemnly, "I owe you another lifetime of servitude."

"And how many are we up to now, James?"

"Six, I think."

"Good, good." Mr. Lewis clapped James on the back fondly. He liked James; he always had, from back when Lisa had been

taller than James. "You should date him," Mr. Lewis would say
to Lisa, who would groan, properly appalled by her father (A)
commenting on her dating life, and (B) telling her to date one
of her good friends. When Lisa had finally relented a year ago,
it had been a tossup whether James had been happier than her
father over the news.

"You have money, Princess?"

Lisa nodded, then turned to James. "My purse is upstairs.
Be right back."

She went upstairs and into her bedroom, intending just to
grab her purse and head right back down. But her reflection in
the vanity mirror caught her eye, and once caught, she froze,
helpless.

She saw herself there in the glass, the Lisabeth Lewis that
she hated more than anything else: fat and scared, desperately
attempting to mask her flaws with baggy clothing and a glint of
makeup. Even with the jacket on, she couldn't disguise her
bulk, the sheer heaviness of her frame. God, how could she
think to leave the house looking like this?

On her dressing table, her wide-handled brush lay like a
discarded magic wand. Lisa snatched it and began to brush her
hair—long strokes, from root to tip, counting with every movement. One hundred strokes would get her hair gleaming. One
hundred strokes would keep James's attention on her face and
away from her bloated body. Yes, one hundred strokes would
save her. That, and maybe different earrings. Maybe the diamond studs her parents had given her for her sixteenth birth-
day. Or perhaps the understated gold hoops. No, wait, she
should wear the silver snowflake drops that James had given her
for Valentine's Day. Yes, he'd like that . . .

She realized she'd lost track of what brushstroke she was up to. Grimacing, she started over.

At fifty-three, there came a knock on her open door. In the mirror, she saw James standing in the doorway, his brow creased, his expression puzzled.

"Leese? Thought you were grabbing your purse."

"Just have to finish my hair," she said, determined not to lose count.

"It looks great."

"I need another minute."

"All right." He entered her room without asking, but after knowing her for so long, he didn't really need her permission.

She watched his reflection sit on her bed and she wondered at the troubled look in his eyes.

"Maybe we could get something to eat before we go to the movie," he said gamely. "Grab some fries at the diner."

Sixty-one. Sixty-two. She could drink water and get a head of iceberg lettuce, no dressing. *Sixty-four, sixty-five.* "Sure."

"You'd be okay with that?"

"Why wouldn't I be?" That had come out defensive. Angrily, she kept brushing. *Seventy. Seventy-one.*

There was a long pause before James spoke. "I just don't want to upset you again, that's all."

"Why would going out to a diner upset me?"

"It wouldn't. You're right. I'm sorry."

She kept brushing. "Okay then."

There was another pause, longer this time. "Suzanne called me. Told me she's worried about you."

Lisa waited until she reached one hundred brushstrokes before she responded. "I don't care what she has to say."

"She thinks you're not eating."

"She's wrong." God knew, Lisa ate. She ate too damn much. That's why she looked so fat in everything she wore. She set down the brush, then fumbled through her jewelry drawer for the silver earrings.

As she put them on, James said, "You know you're my girl, right?"

"Sure." She even managed a smile.

"And you can talk to me. About anything. You know that, right?"

Her smile slipped a little. "I know." They'd always talked, way before they'd ever kissed. There was a time when Lisa would have sworn James had known her better than she'd known herself. But that was before the Thin voice. And no matter how much she cared for James, and he for her, she could never tell him about *that*. "I really love these earrings," she said brightly, her smile back on, full wattage.

"They look terrific on you." James stood up and walked over to her, until he was standing behind her. Wrapping his arms around her waist, he leaned his chin down on her shoulder and hugged her, gently, as if he were afraid of crushing her. "Leese," he said softly, "you know if there was a problem or anything, you know I'm here for you. Don't you?"

An old-fashioned set of scales shone brightly in Lisa's mind, momentarily blinding her to her obsession over her weight. She thought about telling James her dream, the horse, the Scales.

And decided against it. It was bad enough that one day, James would wake up and realize he was wasting his time with her. The last thing she should do was let him know she was probably certifiable.

||||||

In the garden, the black horse was joined by a pale horse. The two steeds munched on rhododendrons and swished their tales. A few adventuresome mosquitoes buzzed near their rumps and then settled down for a nibble. A moment later, a cluster fell to the ground, starved and dying. The rest simply fell down dead.

The Pale Rider stood beneath Lisabeth's window, unseen, listening to the girl talk with the boy. After a few minutes, the Rider sighed.

"Sure," Death said to no one in particular. "And the others call *me* a slacker."

CHAPTER 4

Even before she accidentally turned the food to ash, Lisa knew that going to the diner was a mistake.

It had been the smell. Walking through those double doors, Lisa had been hit with a wave of aroma that made her mouth water and her head spin. Joe's was a greasy spoon of a diner, with burgers that dripped juices as you bit into them and fries that were to die for. She remembered the smells, the tastes, so much more.

She and James when they're just friends, sitting with Suzanne and the others in their usual group, all laughing about the stupid horror movie they just saw, and James is taking french fries and pretending they're fangs and he makes like he's going to bite Lisa's neck and she's howling with laughter . . .

Smelling those burgers, those hedonistic french fries, sent Lisa's self-control into a tailspin as she walked with James to their usual booth in the corner. By the time they were seated, her willpower had crashed and burned.

She and James, newly dating, strolling through the diner door hand in hand and Suzanne leading the chorus of "About Time" and Lisa's cheeks heating because everyone's looking at her differently than before and she sees two popular girls rolling their eyes as if to say, "What does he see in her?" and she feels fat for the first time ever as James dangles a cheese fry over her open mouth . . .

When the waitress came over, James ordered the cheese fries

and a Cherry Coke. Lisa primly requested lettuce and a Diet Coke, but her heart was cannonballing in a pool of hot oil and frying potatoes.

She and James sitting in the corner booth, their booth, and she snaps at James as he eats his fries because God it's so unfair that guys can just eat and eat and eat and not gain a pound, but James doesn't know she's upset about the food so he snaps back and they get into their first fight right there in the diner in front of everyone . . .

Lisa sipped her calorie-free soda and told herself she could have one cheese fry. Just one. She could do a couple hundred sit-ups when she got home. She'd have one fry, and that would both satisfy her screaming taste buds and mollify James, who'd already said they could split his order. In fact, he'd seemed glad that she was interested in food at all.

Of course he is, she thought darkly. Guys always thought with their stomachs. And Suzanne—former friend Suzanne, *ex*-friend Suzanne—had all but poisoned James into thinking that Lisa wasn't eating. Yes, Lisa decided: just one fry would do wonders, for Lisa and James both.

You're weak, the Thin voice scolded.

Lisa wavered. *It's just one.*

It's dripping with grease. Yellow, nasty grease that will coat your thighs and butt and hips, and add to the wings under your arms.

Lisa imagined the cheese fry, pictured dipping it into a blob of catsup. She practically tasted the heady combination of starch and sweetness and salt, covered with slick, bubbly cheese, slightly browned.

Her stomach gurgled.

Panicked, she covered her belly with her hand to muffle the

sound. James didn't notice, thank God. He sat across from her, smiling, his posture relaxed, except for the tiny ridge between his eyes. Lisa thought of it as his worry line. It almost made her laugh: here she was, on the verge of a breakdown over the Pavlovish power of french fry odor, but James was the one worrying. About her, probably. At times, he could be so overprotective.

Well, one fry would soothe his fears. That would prove she wasn't some basket case, no matter what her so-called friend Suzanne had to say.

The Thin voice sniffed its derision. *You're weak. You're fat because you're weak.*

Over her stomach, Lisa's hand balled into a fist. Her nails bit into the meat of her palm, and through the pain she told herself not to cry—not in front of James, out here where everyone could see. The diner was crowded—it was Saturday night, after all, and everyone knew that Joe's had the best cheap food in town. They'd said hi to a handful of kids from school, all hanging out at the diner until it was time to hit the movies, or the pool hall, or the bowling alley. Too many people were here. Lisa absolutely, positively couldn't cry. God, she wanted to go home.

"Hey," James said, his voice startled. "What's wrong?"

She painted on a smile. "Nothing."

"You look upset."

"I'm good," she said, just as her phone buzzed. She slipped it out of her pocket and saw that it was a message from Tammy:

UR BOY IS HAWT

Lisa glanced around until she spotted Tammy four tables down, sitting with about ten other people. She texted back:

HE IS

She didn't have anything else to say, so she let it go at that. Knowing Tammy was in the diner made her rethink the french fry choice. Lisa should've known the other girl would be here; Tammy came to Joe's often. But then, Tammy's house was not even two minutes away; she didn't have to worry about public stalls to take care of her snacking. It certainly saved her from having to bring a barf bag with her.

Lisa sipped her diet soda and fretted. If only she had as much control as Tammy. If only she could bring herself to vomit, she wouldn't be sitting here, freaking out over one stupid cheese fry.

You're weak, the Thin voice said again. And Lisa agreed.

Another buzz. This time, the message said:

WHAT R U GONNA EAT?

Lisa texted back:

LETTUCE & DC

James slurped his soda, probably because he knew it annoyed her. He asked, "Who's texting you when you're out on such a hot date?"

"It's just Tammy."

"Ah."

That one word held a dictionary's worth of meaning, rang-ing from "I forgot you're friends with her" to "She's nasty." James didn't like Tammy. Lisa couldn't fathom why. Tammy was funny and smart and understanding. Anger bubbled in Lisa's belly. At times, James could be so mean.

But he was a guy. Guys didn't get things the way girls did; the way Tammy did, anyway. Tammy was a good friend—her best friend. Faithful—completely unlike Suzanne.

Buzz. Lisa glanced at her phone. The message read:

UR SO GOOD

That made Lisa smile. Fortified with Tammy's approval, Lisa sipped her Diet Coke. No french fry for her. Soon they'd leave Joe's and be on their way to the movie. In the darkness of the theater, she'd sit with James's hand in hers and her head on his shoulder, and for that little pocket of time, she'd be com-forted and safe from everything, from the Thin voice and her own scorn. She'd watch the movie, and she'd be happy, if only for a little while.

James said something funny, and Lisa laughed. His worry line eased, and the two fell into the dating routine they had perfected over the past year. Lisa allowed herself to relax. It looked like she was going to make it through the diner test.

But then the plate of fries arrived, dripping with melted cheese. Lisa's bowl of iceberg wedges looked washed out and sickly compared to the golden hues of the cheese fries—the white gold of the cheddar, steaming and decadent; the sun-tanned strips of potato, sizzling, enticing.

Oh God.

Lisa forked lettuce into her mouth and didn't taste the crispness of the leaves as she chewed. She tried not to stare at the platter of french fries as her sensory glands overloaded.

James drowned the fries in catsup, then picked up a mutilated shoestring, heavy with cheese and dripping red. He shoved it into his mouth indelicately, made sounds of animal pleasure as he worked his jaw, chewing. His Adam's apple bobbed as he swallowed.

"Man," he said with a grin, "I forgot how good these can be. Here, try one."

Her breath caught in her throat. Keeping her smile frozen on her face, she took her fork and stabbed a fry, then deposited it on her plate, near the edge so it wouldn't touch the lettuce. Picking up her knife, she cut the fry into cubes, and then again into smaller cubes. And then she took a sip of diet soda, and smiled even bigger at James, and she proceeded not to eat the fry she so desperately wanted to put into her mouth.

James talked to her, and she made all the appropriate sounds and head motions, but for the life of her, Lisa couldn't have told you what he was talking about. It was as if his words were coming to her from under water—thick, distorted, rolling away before the sounds made sense. All she could think about was the french fry, and how she wanted it and hated it and wished it would just go away.

In her mind, she saw a set of gleaming bronze scales . . . and then her vision went black.

She gasped, and then a coughing fit seized her, shredding the blackness with every choked-off wheeze.

"Leese?" James's voice sounded concerned. "You okay?"

No, you idiot, I'm not okay. I'm choking. But Lisa couldn't speak, so she nodded, tears welling up in the corners of her eyes, and she took some hasty sips of Diet Coke. Once she could find her voice, she said, "Just swallowed wrong."

"Can happen when you eat too fast."

Great, now he was mocking her. She drank more soda and tried not to hate James, sitting there so smugly, so untouched by the powerful aroma of cheese fries. She sipped, realizing that at least when food was involved, she was able to feel. Maybe the emotion was bitter and hateful, but it was better than the vacuum she otherwise seemed to dwell in.

Food was real. Everything else paled.

"Damn, I'm starving."

James's voice snapped her out of her bleak thoughts, and she saw him shovel in mouthful after mouthful of french fries. It was disgusting and fascinating, a culinary car wreck that she couldn't tear her gaze from. He slobbered; he snuffled. Her boyfriend was a pig. Who was the witch that turned men into hogs? Circe? Medea? One of those Greek villainesses, wasn't it? At that moment, Lisa completely related.

Not pausing to swallow, he said, "Want another before I finish them all?"

God, he was torturing her. She was about to say something harmless, such as she wanted to finish her lettuce first, but then she glanced down at her own plate, and her voice failed her.

The diced-up fry was gone. In its place was a streak of fine black ash, as if someone had scraped the burned part off toast and dumped it on her plate. Most of the lettuce was gone, too;

some wilted pieces remained, as far from the scorched bits as possible.

She didn't realize her hand was shaking until she dropped her fork. Lisa swallowed thickly as she retrieved the utensil from the table, and damned if she didn't have the taste of cheese fries in her mouth.

Well, cheese fries and lettuce. Two great tastes that went great together.

"Lisa," James said, "your face just turned green."

"Did it?" Her voice sounded far away and tinny, as if she were hearing a poor recording.

"Yeah." He reached over and touched her forehead. "And you're sweating. You sure you're feeling okay?"

"Just fine," she said faintly, staring at the plate where her french fry and lettuce had, apparently, disintegrated.

That was insane. That was ludicrous. Food didn't just vanish, poof, all gone.

In her mind, she heard a cold voice whisper from the depths of a nightmare: *"Thou art Famine."*

She stared at her plate.

"Lisa?"

"Excuse me," she said, then stumbled off to the ladies' room to vomit. Tammy would have been proud.

||||||

By Lisa's garden, the black horse and pale horse were joined by a white horse. The remaining mosquitoes had learned their lesson and stayed far, far away as the steeds continued to graze.

The White Rider said nothing as the Pale Rider strummed on an acoustic guitar, playing a soul-rending tune that mixed hope and despair in equal portions. Death sang, the words written by a singer long dead. Soon the music stopped, and the last line was sung. Only then did Pestilence speak.

"All in all," he said, "is all we are? Does that even make sense?"

Death grinned at him. "It does if you have the soul of a poet."

Pestilence sighed. Death, he'd learned long ago, was weird. "So, how fares our newest comrade?"

"She's having dinner."

"She's . . ." The White Rider's words faded, and he stared owlishly at the Pale Rider. "Surely, you're joking."

"Nope. She's conflicted."

"You don't say." Pestilence spat; where his spittle landed, the ground sizzled and smoked. "So, what are you doing?"

"Waiting."

"Of course," the White Rider said dryly. "You're so very good at that."

Death shrugged. "Why be impatient? They all come to me, in their time."

That made Pestilence nod. At the end of it all, even he, finally, would be subject to Death's cold touch. With his luck, that fateful day would be long and long away. He shouldered his bow, one that needed neither string nor arrow. "I have to go; South Africa has another virus brewing."

"You'll stop by to say your hellos when you're through?"

That wasn't really a question, no matter how it was phrased. "Of course." Pestilence paused, and the silver crown on his brow gleamed in the moonlight. "Has *she* shown up?"

Death shook his head. "Not yet. But she will, no matter how much she wants to stay away. It's in her nature to cause trouble."

"Indeed." The White Rider inclined his head. "Until next time."

"Go thee out unto the world," Death intoned, granting his colleague the proper dismissal. And then he added, "And try to have some fun while you're at it."

Pestilence rolled his eyes. Yes, Death was very weird.

||||||

"For the last time," Lisa growled, "I'm fine. Let's go to the stupid movie."

"You're *not* fine." James wasn't yelling exactly, but he wasn't talking in his normal laid-back voice, either. They sat in his car, still in the parking spot outside the diner, fighting over whether she should go home. "You just vomited in the bathroom."

"Something I ate didn't agree with me," she said for the third time.

"Yeah." He looked at her, his eyes searching, his mouth pressed into a grim line. "You said."

She couldn't take his silent judgment. "What?"

"You tell me, Leese. You barely eat, and then when you do eat something, you run to the bathroom to puke. What do *you* think?"

"I think," she said tightly, her teeth clenched, "I have a stomach bug or something."

"Or something." He stopped talking as he regarded her, his gaze burning, even though his eyes were sad.

"*What?* Come on, James. Tell me what you're thinking."

He looked away from her, staring straight ahead, not answering her.

Frustrated, Lisa mimicked his posture, staring vacantly through the windshield. Outside, kids meandered in the parking lot, chatting and laughing and high-fiving, all so natural, so easy. None of them had to gird themselves as if for war when they stepped outside, making sure they were fortified with control techniques and visions of perfection to keep them motivated and sane. None of them understood how dangerous it was to be around food, to wage a constant battle of willpower—and how easy it would be to just surrender and lose oneself completely. No, they were blind, and deaf, and they parroted the latest lines from the latest magazines, all full of promises of health and beauty and attractiveness.

All stuffed with lies.

When James finally spoke, his voice was both soft and hard, quiet and yet terribly firm. "Are you bulimic?"

The question so startled her that she let out a laugh. Her? Bulimic? She couldn't even manage to stick her fingers down her throat. "No, of course not. That's just gross." Yes, that too.

He turned to face her, and she noticed the worry line nestled between his brows. "You promise me? You really just had to puke before because, what, something disagreed with you?"

"Promise." Really, it was sort of sweet how concerned he was. She smiled broadly, and never mind how it hurt her cheeks. "I'm okay. Maybe I'm coming down with something. That's probably why I've been so tired, and now with what just happened at the diner . . ." Her mind fixed on the ashes on her plate, but she pushed that thought away. "I'm probably getting the flu."

A very long pause before a relieved smile flitted across his lips. "Okay then." But the smile vanished, and he looked unconvinced.

Damn that Suzanne, putting such stupid ideas into his head!

"I'm still up for a movie," she said brightly, trying to convince him that she was still a good girlfriend. "We could even see that new one you've been talking about. You know, the one with all the gore and blood." She hated horror films, hated seeing killers wielding improbable weapons and slicing off people's limbs. But for James, she'd do it.

He shook his head as he started the engine. "Uh-uh. If you've got something that's making you puke, I'm getting you home. You should be in bed."

Deflating, Lisa looked down at her lap. "Sorry."

"Not a big deal," he said as he backed out of their spot.

"It was probably the Chinese food I had with Dad before," she said, feeling lame. "Maybe it was undercooked or something."

"Could be."

They rode back to her house in uncomfortable silence—James obviously wrestling with dark thoughts, and Lisa fretting over the way James was acting. When they pulled into her driveway, she was all but in tears.

"I'm sorry," she said, her voice hitching. "I've ruined everything."

He smiled—such a beautiful smile—and reached over to stroke her hair. "Don't be stupid. I just want you healthy." He emphasized the last word, and he caught her gaze, holding it. "You know I love you, right?"

Biting her lip, she nodded. "Love you, too."

"Leese," he said, drinking her in. "If you need anything, you'll tell me, won't you?"

She nodded again.

"Promise?"

"Promise."

"Okay then." He leaned over and kissed her brow, making Lisa feel like a little girl. "Go on in and get some rest. I'll call you tomorrow."

"Okay," she said, and then added, "I baked cookies for you. Let me run in and get them."

"No, don't. If you're up for it, I can come by tomorrow and get them, maybe stay for a while. Bring you some chicken soup," he said, grinning.

Chicken soup, the Thin voice said. *One cup. Two hundred calories. Ninety minutes on the bike.*

She tried to smile, but it faltered around the edges. "I'd like that," she lied.

They said their good nights, and Lisa slunk into her house.

A minute after Lisa shut her front door, a very troubled James drove away.

|||||

"What do you think?" Death asked. "Should I give her five minutes? Let her calm down first? Maybe give her some time to get ready for her big night out? Or should I throw her to the metaphorical wolves?"

The black horse flicked its ears. The pale horse snorted.

"You're right," Death said. "Girls take forever to get ready. I'll go get her."

But he took his time, first stretching out the kinks in his neck and shoulders from hunching over to play his guitar. As he'd said to the White Rider, there really was no need to rush. Starvation was a slow process. Taking an extra minute to collect Famine wouldn't make any difference at all.

Besides, if the new Famine had a heart attack, that would put a damper on his entire evening. Better to let the girl calm down.

Whistling, Death put away his guitar.

CHAPTER 5

Leaning against the front door, Lisa blew out a shaky breath and mopped her forehead. She was having a truly terrible night, and she couldn't even blame PMS; she hadn't gotten her period in two months. (Last month, she'd quietly freaked out when she'd realized she was late, but two over-the-counter tests had proven she wasn't pregnant. She figured it was just a blip in her menstrual cycle, probably due to stress. God knew, she had more than enough stress to deal with.)

Yes, tonight was right up there on the suckascope, as Tammy would have said. Between the instant ashing of the food at the diner and James asking her if she was secretly making herself vomit, it was all Lisa could do not to scream. Her heart was jackhammering in her chest, and she was finding it hard to take a full breath. *Maybe I should take one of Mom's Lexapros,* she thought, yanking her hair away from her face, *or a cup of tea. I have to calm down.*

From upstairs: "Princess? That you?"

"Hey, Dad." The sound of his voice was enough to kick Lisa into routine. She stripped off her jacket and hung it in the front closet, even though she was cold. She would have kept her jacket on, but she didn't want her father to worry. He was a man who liked everything in its place. Dishes belonged in the cupboard; jackets belonged in the closet. She closed the closet door, deciding that a hot cup of chamomile would be divine. And maybe it would even get her warm again.

"You're home early," her father called down. "Everything all right?"

"Not feeling so great, so James brought me back."

She headed into the kitchen, and a minute later, her father joined her. As she stood by the sink to fill the kettle, she noticed that her dad was clearly well into his third glass of vodka on the rocks—his eyes were beady and red rimmed, and he looked like a breath of air would knock him over. Lisa didn't begrudge his drinking; heck, it was Saturday night, and he wasn't driving anywhere.

"What's wrong, honey? Boy, you look pale." Her father touched a hand to her forehead, and she did her best not to flinch. Lisa wasn't a touchy-feely sort of girl. Hugs were rare in her family. And it had taken her weeks of dating James to get comfortable with his casual touches. Lately, being physical with him was an exercise in method acting. It wasn't that she didn't enjoy what they did together, but rather that she simply couldn't believe that he *wanted* to be together with her. Every time James touched her, Lisa had to pretend that she was worthy of his affection. It was exhausting.

"A bit of a stomach thing," she told her father, setting the kettle on the stovetop.

"Mmm. No fever." Mr. Lewis removed his hand, and Lisa released a breath. "Well," he said, "'tis the season for the flu. I'm sorry your night got cut short."

She turned the fire on the burner. "It's okay. I'm going to go to bed early."

"Smart. Want some of the evil pink stuff to coat your stomach?"

Lisa made a face.

"Yeah," her dad said, laughing, "I don't blame you. Still, it might help."

Meh. "Pass, thanks."

"If you change your mind, it's in the medicine cabinet."

She was about to comment along the lines of *Where else would medicine be?* when the phone rang. Lisa grabbed it before her father could blink. "Hello?"

"Lisabeth," her mother said, sounding surprised and, unless Lisa was mistaken, a little put off. "I'm surprised you're home."

In other words, Lisa was a loser. Shrinking from the quiet accusation, Lisa mumbled, "Not feeling well."

"I'm sorry to hear that, dear."

A pause followed as Lisa waited for her mother to ask what was wrong and Mrs. Lewis waited for Lisa to ask how her trip was. After a full thirty seconds had passed, Lisa's mother sighed. "Is your father there?"

"Sure."

"Put him on, please. I'll see you tomorrow, dear."

"Okay." Lisa shoved the receiver at her father, then shut off the burner with a violent twist of her hand. Her father bleated at her mother, all *Yes, dear* and *Of course, dear,* getting whittled away more and more with every token sound of acquiescence.

Lisa fled.

She yanked open the basement door and nearly jumped down the stairs. The finished basement was her sanctuary: by the back wall, the stationary bicycle—complete with its heart rate monitor and calorie index—waited patiently for her supplication. Exercise was her release, her retreat, her salvation. She worshiped here every day, twice a day. Lisa grabbed her iPod from its charger and coded her workout playlist, then climbed onto the exercise bike and began her ritual of sweat— to hell with her cashmere sweater and boots. It didn't matter what she wore; as long as she wore herself out, she would be fine.

Two songs into her workout, her father climbed down the stairs. "Princess," he called out, "you sure you should be exercising if you're not feeling well?"

"Exercise kills germs," she said over the blare of music.

Her dad wasn't convinced. "I don't think it's a good idea for you to push yourself so hard."

"I'm taking it easy, I promise." And she was—instead of her usual hour on the bike, she was limiting it to forty-five minutes. She had increased the level of the program, but she decided not to tell her father that part.

Maybe he would have argued the point if he hadn't just gotten browbeaten by her mom. Instead of pushing back, he said, "Well, all right. I'm heading back upstairs. You know where I am if you need me."

Sure—her father would be heading for a fourth vodka-rocks in a little bit. Lisa wasn't about to interrupt his buzz; God knew, the man deserved a little happiness while his wife was away.

Thinking about her mother, Lisa gritted her teeth and kicked her workout up a notch. The fourth song came on, loud and proud, and Lisa pushed herself to go even faster. She was so into the burning feeling in her thighs that she didn't notice the temperature drop, nor the subtle change of the lighting.

But when Death spoke, she noticed.

"Seriously now," he said, "*this* is how you calm down?"

Lisa jumped out of her seat from the sound of the inhumanly cold voice, and she whirled around to see the delivery man from last night's dream. She recognized him—the long blond hair that hung in his face, the soulful eyes, the scruff of fuzz that framed his mouth and jaw, emphasizing the cleft in his chin. No uniform for him tonight, though; he wore a red and black striped sweater that looked like something James's horror movie killer would sport, and faded blue jeans that showed his legs to be longer and thinner than Lisa's. Sneakers clad his feet—old-fashioned Converse high tops, untied. He was standing by the stairs, arms crossed casually, a relaxed grin on his face.

Two thoughts struck her immediately: first, that she *knew* him, and not just from last night's dream—it was more like a nagging feeling that he looked like a movie star or a rock star, someone whose picture she'd seen before; and second, he absolutely terrified her. He looked human—actually, he looked sexy—but there was no way he was human. Deep in her heart, she knew this.

"I mean, really," he said. "Don't you think the tea would have been the better way to go? Less smelly, for one thing."

The insult shocked her out of her stunned fear, and she spluttered, "Who the hell are you? What are you doing in my house?"

He laughed softly, his eyes twinkling, and he shook his head. "Really now, Lisabeth. You know who I am."

She opened her mouth to say she most certainly did not, and never mind that he looked familiar because she'd never seen him before, not really, when suddenly it clicked. Humans have a race memory, or if you wanted to get Jungian, a collective unconscious—the feelings and experiences that we as a species have learned throughout the ages. In our souls, we recognize the angels and demons that walk among us, as well as the Old Ones who fall in between those categories. In that moment, Lisabeth Lewis recognized Death—even in his current form, which bore more than a passing resemblance to a dead alternative rock singer.

Lisa's eyes widened as recognition set in, and her breath strangled in her throat. Her legs went rubbery, and she collapsed against the exercise bike, thinking, *Oh God oh God oh God oh God—*

Death let out a sigh. "Come on, now. I'm not Him."

She blinked, his words startling her out of her fear. "Who?"

"God."

"G—" She stopped, and her eyes narrowed. "You read my mind?"

"Not that hard to do, especially when you're mentally babbling in terror." He smiled. It was a warm smile, which offset the cold tone of his voice. "No worries, though. I get that reaction a lot."

"Uh-huh." Okay, so Death was talking to her in the finished basement of her house. Right. "Um, what do you want?"

"Me? World peace. A cure for cancer. Food for the hungry." He let out a chuckle. "Okay, no, I'm kidding. What I want, Lisabeth, is for you to stop stalling and take up the mantle of Famine, like you said you'd do."

"The mantle of . . ." *Oh God, the dream.* And more than the dream: the black horse; the Scales on the kitchen table; the food in the diner. It all came rushing back, and Lisa crashed to her knees as her mind overloaded.

Time stretched, and for a very long moment, Lisa drowned in panic. Finally, a cold, thin hand offered her a lifeline; it rested on her shoulder, lightly, and squeezed, providing some small measure of comfort (albeit cold comfort).

Blinking, Lisa looked up and saw Death smiling at her. The part of her ruled by hormones couldn't help but notice how damn cute he was. The rest of her screamed that her hormones had a, ha-ha, death wish.

"Come on, Lisabeth," Death said, not unkindly. "It's time to do your job."

CHAPTER 6

The words didn't make any sense. "My job?" Lisa said as Death helped her to her feet. She was a seventeen-year-old high school junior in the suburbs; she didn't have a *job*.

"Thou art Famine, yo," Death said. "Time to make with the starvation."

Lisa took a shaky breath. "Look. Ah, I think we had a mis-understanding."

The life slowly bled out of Death's face, leaving it pale and terrifying. So very softly, he replied, "Did we now?"

She swallowed, nodded.

He cocked his head and regarded her thoughtfully. "Let's see," Death said, tapping his chin. "Did the misunderstanding happen as you were overdosing on your mother's antidepres-sants? Or was it sometime after that?"

Lisa bit her lip and looked at her feet.

"Because, if you prefer, I can put you back where I found you," Death said. "Overdosing. You'd taken three pills when I rang your doorbell. You had twenty-four to go. And then I would have come for you anyway, minus the job offer. Is that what you want, Lisabeth?"

She didn't answer.

"Tell me," Death said, no longer sounding thoughtful. "Do you still want to die? I'm happy to oblige."

Lisa squeezed her eyes closed and desperately prayed for this to be a nightmare.

"Lisa? Do you still want to die?"

Did she?

Last night, she'd wanted to just slip into sleep and never wake up. She'd just been so tired of not feeling anything except a dull ache in her chest, a pang for something lost that she truly believed she would never find again. She was tired of either walking on eggshells with James or fighting with him, knowing in her heart that he cared for her and that it didn't matter. She was tired of her parents either coddling her or ignoring her. She was tired of trying to be considerate. And she was so damn tired of the Thin voice telling her that she wasn't good enough, that she was fat, that she would never be happy as long as she still had weight to lose. When you're that tired, sometimes all you want to do is sleep.

But a tiny part of her—the part that cared for James as much as he cared for her, the part that missed Suzanne and loved her mom and dad and hoped that someday she really would be happy even if she never lost all the weight—didn't want to just curl up and die.

Last night, that part of her had been buried too deep for her to remember. But now, with Death standing before her, Lisa felt that small part of her soul, and she tried to hold on to it with arthritic fingers that scrabbled for purchase. As hope slipped away, the Thin voice laughed at her, mocking her as she spiraled deeper into despair.

"Lisa," Death said again, "do you want to die?"

Her voice the barest of whispers, she replied, "I don't know."

Silence stretched between them as Lisabeth Lewis stood before Death, her eyes shut tight and her thoughts a whirling dervish in her mind, and Death loomed over her, considering.

Finally, he said, "Well, until you tell me definitively that yes, you're ready to shuffle off this mortal coil, you're the new Famine."

His declaration echoed in her head and weighed heavily in her heart. "That's it, then?" she said. "Either I'm Famine, or you're going to kill me?"

He let out a laugh, and it echoed in the finished basement. "If you want to get all melodramatic about it, that's one way of looking at it. But you know, I probably wouldn't kill you."

She opened her eyes and stared at Death. "Oh?"

"War would be happy to do it for me." He shrugged, an easy movement of his shoulders. "She has a thing for killing."

Lisa felt the blood drain from her face. "Oh."

"She can be brutal, too," Death added, his voice still cold and yet somehow chipper. "Some people like quick deaths. War isn't one of them. She likes to draw it out. Slowly. And rather painfully."

Lisa's stomach dropped to her toes. For the second time that night, she thought she was going to vomit.

Death grinned. "So chin up, Black Rider. It's time for you to start earning your keep."

|||||||

"Your steed awaits," Death said.

In the garden, Lisa tentatively approached the black horse. The good news for her sanity was that the horse—stallion?

mare? gelding? She wasn't about to look between its legs to check—was indeed real, down to its glowing white eyes. The bad news, of course, was that it was the steed of Famine, and Lisa was its designated rider. That part she was still having trouble with.

A horse, she thought, looking at it. She'd never been horseback riding and didn't know the first thing about how to groom such a creature. Did it have to go for walks? Was she supposed to brush its mane? Feed it apples? Where was she supposed to stable it? And what on earth would her parents say? They never even let her have any pets after she'd accidentally killed her goldfish when she was seven. She hadn't believed her mom when she'd warned Lisa that overfeeding the fish would kill them. A quarter jar of food later, Lisa had a tankful of belly-up golden red fish. She'd cried, and her dad had patted her shoulder as her mom unceremoniously dumped the dead fish down the toilet.

She had a feeling her parents wouldn't be too keen on an equestrian pet, especially one that ate her mom's rhododendrons.

Not knowing the proper way to introduce herself without spooking the black horse, she offered her hand for it to sniff. The horse deigned to do so, then kneeled down before her, its ears pulled forward, as if expecting something. A treat, maybe.

Lisa stood there stupidly, shivering in the cold.

"Famine, your steed is waiting for you to climb up," Death said, sounding jovial.

With a shaking hand, Lisa reached out to stroke the black horse's side. Its flesh felt surprisingly warm, almost as if it hungered for her touch. As she glided her fingers over its hide, the horse nickered softly. Encouraged by the sound, Lisa stroked it again.

"What's its name?" she asked, her voice filled with wonder.

"Our steeds have no names," Death said. "They simply are, much as we are."

She glanced over her shoulder to look at the Pale Rider. "I have a name. Don't you?"

He smiled, bemused. "You were Lisabeth Lewis. Now you are Famine."

She didn't like the past tense usage with her name, but she decided that correcting Death was a bad idea. "So who were you before you were . . . you?"

His smile stretched wider. "I have always been what I am."

"You never had a name?"

"Oh, I've had hundreds of names. Thousands. People have a penchant for naming things. It gives them a sense of control, of understanding." He spread his arms wide. "But no matter what I am called, I am universal. I don't need a name."

Lisa thought about that as she stroked the horse. "I think that's sad," she said. "Everyone should have a name."

"So, what will you name your steed?"

The horse turned its head to regard her, and she was struck by the frank curiosity she saw in its white eyes.

"I think . . . I'd like to call you Midnight," she said to the horse, understanding on some level that she should ask the steed for permission to give it a name. "Would that be all right?"

The horse nickered again, and Lisa thought its mouth quirked into a smile.

"Well," Death said, "at least you didn't go with Muffin."

The horse—Midnight—cast a long look at the Pale Rider, then snorted.

Lisa bit back a laugh. Oh, she liked this horse. "People can't see it," she said to Death, "can they?"

"Only Horsemen can see steeds. Come on now. Saddle up."

As there was no saddle, Lisa said to the horse, "May I pull myself up?"

And damned if the horse didn't nod.

"Okay," she said, and then said "okay" again. She took a deep breath, and then grabbed hold of Midnight's black mane and pulled herself up, launching her left leg over the horse's back. She wobbled for a moment, but soon she was sitting astride the massive black beast. A wave of delight washed over her, leaving her giddy.

Then the horse stood up, and Lisa let out a squeak. She gripped its mane for dear life.

"My dad's going to worry," she said over the clamor of her galloping heartbeat. "If I'm not there and he checks on me, he's going to absolutely freak out."

"He won't even notice you're gone."

"If James calls . . ."

"No one will call you. You are no longer Lisabeth Lewis. You are Famine."

She turned her head to see that Death, too, was atop his steed. "But I don't know what to do or where I'm supposed to go!"

Seated on his pale horse, Death looked at ease, all slouching confidence and careless smiles. His long blond hair rustled in the wind. "Your steed knows where Famine is supposed to be," he said. "As for what to do, you'll need your symbol of office."

"My . . . ?" Oh, right. "The Scales."

"Yes."

"They're inside."

"No," Death said patiently, "they're not."

Lisa took a breath and held it, wondering what she was supposed to do. She remembered the feel of the metal balance in her hands last night, pictured the way the light gleamed off the plates earlier that evening when the Scales had appeared on the kitchen table.

Exhaling, she held out her hand and thought: *Come.* She felt incredibly stupid, but she thought it again, more clearly: *Come to me.*

She'd expected maybe a poof of smoke, even a boom. But the Scales materialized quietly before her, something out of nothing, hovering in the nighttime air like some clockwork hummingbird. The balance was smaller than she remembered; the whole thing could sit in the palm of her hand.

Scaled according to size, she thought, and nearly laughed.

Hesitating for a moment, Lisa stared at the bronze (or maybe brass) set of scales, impressed by how something so small could radiate such menace. The center beam was intricately shaped, curving and sensuous—rather feminine-looking, except for the harsh, masculine quality to the metal. At its tip was a hook, suitable either for gripping with a hand or attaching to a ring. Identical thin beams stretched from the top of the center post, also curving lazily in S shapes, like a bisected figure eight. Both of those beams ended in metal rings, from which hung a triad of chains. Each of the triads held a metal dish. The Scales were beautiful, and old, almost shining with power.

Lisa steeled herself, then closed her fist around the hook at the tip of the Scales.

In a rush, the world opened its mouth to her—and it was screaming.

Everywhere—the air around her, the ground beneath her, the stars above—rippled with the soul-wrenching cries of hunger: the trees and bushes and plants all twisted and bent, their branches and stems clawing the sky in skeletal panic; the animals and insects, flying and crawling and burrowing, each frantic in its own way, searching incessantly to end the gnawing demand in its belly; the swarms of people, clotting the world, stuffing themselves only to beg for more, be it food or wealth or attention—all of them, desperate, insatiable. So very hungry.

All of them, leeching on to her. Sucking her dry.

"Make it stop!" she screamed. "Oh God, please, make it stop!"

Over the cacophony of every living thing wailing for sustenance, she heard Death speak in a still, small voice: *Balance.*

She shrieked, "I don't understand!"

Death spoke, his voice a velvet murmur in her mind: *Living means constantly growing closer to death. Satisfaction only temporarily relieves hunger. Find the balance, and plant your feet.*

Trembling, Lisa held on to the Scales with both hands. The voice of the world screamed all around her, and it was all she could do to hold on to the Scales and not slam her hands over her ears.

Balance.

Through the turmoil of the hungry, Lisa felt the black horse beneath her, a soothing presence, one that was steady, certain. She heard the quiet assuredness of Death, unmoved in the face of gripping anguish. She took a tortured breath, and then another, and as she breathed and forced herself to simply accept that the world was screaming, those voices soon diminished. They didn't quiet to stillness, nor did they fade; they were a steady hum of background noises, static that she felt with all her senses. It was uncomfortable, like the first stirrings of a migraine. But it was manageable.

Slowly, she lowered the Scales. A moment later, the balance popped away—outside of her vision, yes, but she knew that all she had to do was summon it, and the Scales would appear again. Sort of a negative space. She would have thought it was neat if she weren't on the verge of a complete breakdown.

Looking up, she met Death's dark gaze. "What was that?" she asked, her voice raw.

"That was you fighting against yourself."

"No, that wasn't me. That was . . ." She tried to compress all that she'd felt into words, and she failed miserably. "Every-thing," she said lamely.

"Thou art Famine," Death said. "The voices of the hungry should beckon to you like old friends. They shouldn't cause you pain."

"Those weren't friends." Lisa folded her arms over her chest and hugged herself. Beneath her, Midnight held still, as if the horse sensed that she needed it to be steady for her. "That was overwhelming. The voices—they were everywhere."

Death nodded. "Hunger is part of life. Life is all around you."

"I can't do this," she whispered. Tears welled in her eyes. "Whatever it is you think I agreed to, I can't do it."

"You are full of fear," Death said, "when instead you should be comfortable with your own strength."

That made her bark out a laugh, one utterly without mirth. "I'm not strong." God, no, she wasn't strong. She was weak. Pathetic.

And fat, the Thin voice whispered.

Oh yes, and so very fat.

"You will learn," Death said knowingly, sitting atop the pale horse. "But I'm afraid you'll have to learn on the job. You're running late."

She rubbed her arms. "Where am I going?"

Death motioned broadly, taking in the night. "Out unto the world."

Lisa blinked at him. "Going to be a long night."

He let out a belly laugh, one that was rich and resonating, filling the space between them. "Hey, she *does* have a sense of humor." Death winked at her, and for a moment, Lisa thought she saw a skull peering at her beneath a mask of flesh. "You're starting small. Don't worry. She'll be apples."

Before Lisa could ask what apples had to do with anything, Midnight reared up. With a squawk, Lisa grabbed on to the horse's mane, terrified she was going to fall. A wild part of her wanted to shout, *Hiyo, Silver, awayyyy!* The rest of her screamed that she was insane, that this whole thing was insane, that the world no longer made sense.

And then they were gone.

Chapter 7

The world before her blurred like half-forgotten memories, all browns and greens and blues, smeared in a finger-painted landscape. Faster than wind, truer than love, they traveled across the land and sea, dusting mountains, skimming clouds. On they went, thundering like impending doom: Famine of the Apocalypse and her black steed.

Lisabeth Lewis did her best not to vomit.

At first, Lisa was too petrified to do more than hold on for dear life, squeezing her thighs until they were rigid blocks, her eyes shut tight. But within a few minutes of being borne on horseback, she realized she wasn't getting thrown off and trampled, and her stomach settled down. They were galloping through the air like some mythical creatures—and if you wanted to get technical, Lisa now *was* a mythical creature—but the horse's footing was sure. It knew what it was doing. That, Lisa believed.

Slowly, she loosened her death grip, relaxing her knees. The horse, to her extreme relief, rewarded her by smoothing out the ride. There in the sky, Lisa found her balance. Anxiety gradually bled into excitement. Lisa grinned. For the first time in her life, she was riding a horse. And not just any horse—she was atop a mighty steed, soaring beyond where eagles dared.

This, she told herself, *is really freaking cool.*

The horse moved with liquid grace beneath her, and Lisa leaned forward, hugging the steed's powerful neck, feeling Midnight's muscles flowing beneath her body. As the horse carried her, Lisa's fear gave way to trust, and with that came a surge of confidence, a sense of pride so strong that it seared her chest—so very different from the acid pain of heartburn. This was satisfaction that was bone-deep, and it had nothing to do with food.

Her hair whipping in the wind, she let out a whoop of exhilaration, delighting in the sheer joy of the ride.

All too soon, their pace slowed. They galloped over an expanse of dust, the land parched and cracked, and Lisa looked down in dismay, knowing intuitively that once this had been a reservoir. Beyond the brown, they next passed a large body of water, its edge lined with trees—and again, Lisa looked down and despaired, sensing how those trees were stressed and dying, how the content of the water itself had shifted and now was too salty for many of the creatures that depended on it for life. She smelled the memory of brushfires, and the ghost of dust storms assaulted her nostrils. She swallowed, but the taste of eroded soil stayed on her tongue. She felt the echo of weather patterns past and understood that the climate had changed, wreaking havoc on the land. Here, drought reigned supreme.

Lisa's mouth went dry and her stomach cramped. Dizziness slammed into her, knocking her off balance. She gripped Midnight's mane and prayed for the sickness to pass. It didn't, but it became bearable somehow.

Soon they traveled past the wounded land, and Lisa worked saliva down her throat. God, she was so thirsty. All of her days— those endless days—in which she had refused to allow herself to

eat were nothing compared to the overwhelming compulsion for
her to drink. She had to slake her thirst—*had* to.

As if the horse sensed her distress, Midnight shifted slightly
and then arced down. Soon they were over a city by the water:
Lisa saw buildings and bridges and what she thought were is-
lets, with trees dotting the landscape and boats peppering the
water. And she saw people, yes—a flood of people, surging
through land and sea, teeming with life.

Screaming with hunger.

They touched ground outside of a restaurant. Unlike back
home, here it was daylight. Judging from the position of the
sun and the crowd of people on the street, it was lunchtime.

Midnight knelt down, and Lisa leaned forward, then lifted
her left leg over the horse's back so that both of her legs were on
the steed's right side. Feet-first, she slid herself off the horse and
onto the ground. Her knees were a bit wobbly, but all in all, she
thought she dismounted all right—it was her first time, and no
one had helped her. The thought made her grin.

She hugged Midnight's neck. "Thank you," she murmured.

The steed nickered softly, and again Lisa was struck by the
emotion she saw in its white eyes.

Standing tall, she turned to face the doors of the restaurant.
She had no idea what she was supposed to do, but the pang in
her belly and discomfort in her throat told her that before anything else, she needed to drink.

Taking a deep breath, she walked up to the doors—walked
through the doors as if she were a ghost.

Neat, she thought, smiling.

Inside, the place was packed. Patrons sat and ate and talked,
their mouths full of food and conversation, their stomachs

content but their appetites demanding more. Lisa felt them all, their bodies becoming extensions of hers; she felt them stuff themselves far beyond what they required.

They bloated her, distorted her, and she was disgusted. But deeper than the disgust was the need to drink.

Water. Now, or she'd die.

Staggering from the weight of the diners, she picked her way to the nearest table and grabbed a water glass, then drank greedily, the liquid spilling down her chin and wetting her sweater. The couple seated at the table didn't notice her or the missing glass, but the woman suddenly felt dizzy and nearly pitched over in her seat.

"Luv," the man said as Lisa drank, "you look crook."

"Feel like I'm about to chuck," the woman rasped, her body dehydrated.

The man, also suddenly feeling ill, started to sweat. He gulped down his drink.

The woman bolted out of her seat and raced away, a hand covering her mouth.

The man desperately tried to flag down a waiter to get more to drink. He'd never been so thirsty in all his life.

Lisa liked their accents. Maybe British or Scottish or Australian; she couldn't tell. But definitely one of those places, where the words all rolled up and down hills and language turned into something sexy.

Her own thirst quenched, Lisa set down the glass and moved along the aisles of the restaurant. It seemed a well-to-do place, based on the table settings, the way the patrons were dressed, and the manner in which the food was presented on their plates. It was the sort of place where people spent a ton of money and gorged themselves with exotic-sounding meals laden with calories and fat. The Thin voice would have been flummoxed trying to calculate how much exercise time would be necessary to counteract even a single mouthful.

Frowning, Lisa stared at the expensive plates decorated with their expensive foods, at the people—thin and fat and healthy and sickly and all manners in between, all of them dressed to the nines—using the proper utensils to shovel in their salads, to slice their meats, to slather butter on their rolls. So very proper. So very excessive.

So very unlike her.

The stirrings of anger within her eroded her control, and soon the background voices of the world around her shifted, became prominent. Lisa didn't realize she was once again hearing the incessant hunger of life; it had been a subtle change, an undercurrent in her awareness that slowly altered her equilibrium. It was a steady throbbing in her head, a gnawing ache in her belly. She looked at the people around her, lunching.

And she was hungry.

God, she hated them for it. She hated these people who could sit here so easily and navigate their way through their meals so thoughtlessly. Her fists trembled. She looked at them, with their Piri Piri prawns and soft-shell mud crab and rock oysters, their cheese plates decorated with apricots and cucumbers and dates, the bouillabaisse and yuzu sauce. She watched them as they ate, with no concern other than gorging themselves. She listened to the sounds they made, slobbering, slurping, rooting around their plates like pigs and leaving their droppings for servers to trot away. They feasted, oblivious to Lisa's rage.

They ignored her, the same way her mother did.

Lisa narrowed her eyes. No, she wouldn't let them ignore her. She was here among them. She'd announce herself to them, make them see her, make them feel her.

The Scales burned in her mind, and once again the world drowned in blackness as Lisa unleashed the power of Famine. Lost to the darkness, she didn't see the food on the plates disintegrate, but she felt every entrée and appetizer and dessert transform into ash. She spread her arms and the hunger reached out, person by person, touching everyone in the restaurant, from the busboy trying to earn enough money to offset university costs and the assistant manager filling in yet again for the womanizing owner who was off with one of his three mistresses, to every single customer seated and standing and waiting for a table. Stomachs growled. Mouths dried. And tempers shortened.

No one at the restaurant knew what had happened to the food; surely, they must have eaten. But they were miserable, the whole lot of them—and they were utterly ravenous. Waiters pawed through breadbaskets, only to find them empty. In the kitchen, the chefs raided the refrigerators and the pantries, only to be screamed at by the harried assistant manager, who felt the stirrings of a sugar drop. In the dining room, customers began to complain: the portions had been too small; the food hadn't been cooked properly; they never received their orders, and so on. One server, already surly from dieting and loathe to think of the celery sticks and potted cheese that waited, snapped at the patron who was leaving without the courtesy of a tip.

Blood boiled. And soon, fists flew.

The evening news and all the dailies would report it, of course, as a "Food Fight." The net result would be three broken limbs, four concussions, twenty-three lawsuits, two broken chairs, one scathing food review, and the sacking of the assistant manager.

Standing away from the raging people who'd spilled out of the restaurant, witnessing the chaos and now the slowly impending order in the form of police and ambulances and television cameras, Lisa stared in mute horror. At first, after the power of Famine had rolled back inside of her and color had again filled the world, Lisa had been numb, safe in the null void she dwelled in most of the time, cocooned from emotions and consequences. (Even the Thin voice couldn't reach her in that state, one she found easily whenever she exercised herself to the point of exhaustion.) But the shouts and the cries and the incessant chatter of the people near her sent cracks along the edges of that void, and soon feelings leaked through.

There she stood, seeing the results of her handiwork. One of the people getting loaded into an ambulance was a girl younger than Lisa. A table had gotten pushed over, onto her, and had broken her leg. Lisa had felt it. And at the time, she hadn't cared—all that had mattered was showing everyone what it meant to be truly hungry. But now she heard the girl's whimpers and sobs, and she felt the anguish and impotent rage of the girl's parents.

Lisa had done that.

And God, even with the taste of foods too numerous to count somehow on her tongue, even in the face of all the horror she'd just caused, Lisa was hungry.

Her breath started coming too fast, and her throat was far too tight. She needed to climb on her bike and exercise away the guilt; she had to fast, to lock her hunger away. She shivered, colder now than ever before.

She was a monster—as ugly inside as she was outside.

Dizzy, she leaned against Midnight, praying once again for this to be a nightmare. "I can't do this," she whispered.

The horse nickered.

"Tell me," she said, tears stinging her eyes, "what am I supposed to do?"

Perhaps in answer to her plea, the air shifted, bringing with it a sharp smell that made Lisa grimace. It tasted like blood.

It tasted like fear.

"Ah, so *you're* the new one," a woman's voice said—cutting and cruel, a voice meant to stab and leave you bleeding.

Lisa whirled about to see a knight—a for-real *knight,* complete with armor—seated on a rust-colored horse. Sunlight gleamed off the naked sword in the knight's gauntleted fist.

Staring at that shining weapon, Lisa was suddenly very, very afraid.

"Hello, little girl," the knight said, and even though a helmet concealed the speaker's face, Lisa could sense the knight—the woman—grinning hugely. "I'm War."

CHAPTER 8

The woman loomed like a metallic beast, gleaming in silver armor from head to toe. A plume peaked the helmet's top, scarlet as a cardinal's feathers. Her tapered breastplate sported an image of a blood-red sword, its point aimed high as if to challenge God to a duel. Bits of mesh flashed beneath the plates on her shoulders and elbows and knees, winking crimson. Her boots looked big enough to kick down brick walls, and her hands in their gauntlets—one gripping the horse's reins and the other wielding the mighty sword—would have made lumberjacks feel unmanly.

Staring up at the Horseman (Horsewoman? What was the proper gender acknowledgment for a Rider of the Apocalypse?) seated on the massive horse, Lisa swallowed thickly. Dear God, the woman was enormous! It had nothing to do with physical bulk, either, even though she clearly was no lightweight. No, it was the knight's sheer presence. She radiated power like a miniature sun.

It took Lisa several seconds to find her voice. When she finally spoke, the word came out as a breathy whisper. "War?"

"The Red Rider," the woman agreed. Lisa found herself wondering what she looked like beneath the face-covering helmet. "Death's handmaiden," she added with a wry chuckle. "Among other things."

Other . . . ?

Oh!

Lisa thought of some of the things that James did with her when the mood struck him to be amorous—and really, he was a normal seventeen-year-old boy, so that mood happened quite a lot—and she then tried to picture Death doing those things with the armored female knight.

Okay, ew.

The thought of Death and this Junoesque woman doing . . . well, *anything* together was enough to make Lisa want to shower. A lot. Death was sexy (and God, did she need therapy even for thinking something like that; she wasn't even Goth, for goodness' sake) and sort of nice when he wasn't being scary. But *this* woman, doing it with Death? That was just nasty. For one thing, she looked big enough to break Death's back. Wrapping those legs around Death's waist would crush him like a walnut.

Maybe Death liked it rough.

Lots of therapy, Lisa decided. Perhaps War had alluded to her relationship with Death to make Lisa uneasy or jealous. All it did was squick her out. And that, strangely enough, made her feel less scared.

Not quite as intimidated, Lisa remembered her manners. She took a step forward, offering her hand. "Hi."

Midnight bumped Lisa's arm away a moment before the red horse snapped at the space where Lisa's hand had been. Yelping, Lisa jumped back as War's horse tried to bite her again. Midnight stood its ground, baring its teeth. Sharp teeth, Lisa saw, trembling—very, very sharp teeth.

Her horse was *defending* her. A wave of gratitude—unfamiliar and overwhelming—washed over her. Softly she whispered to her steed, "Thank you."

She thought she saw Midnight's nostrils flare, but other than that, it stood its ground, unmoving, boring its white gaze at the red horse. Unafraid. Undaunted.

So unlike Lisa.

The red steed answered the challenge with a snort, its black glowing eyes promising murder. But it didn't move to bite her again.

War threw back her head and roared with laughter. Instead of being muffled by her helmet, her voice seemed to be amplified by the headpiece, and Lisa felt that laugh trip along her spine.

"You don't offer to shake hands in front of a warhorse, girl, let alone War's steed," War declared. "Not unless you want to be called Stumpy."

Blushing furiously, Lisa patted Midnight's neck. She took some comfort from her steed's warmth, and more, oddly enough, from the tension that all but vibrated from Midnight, whose ears were flat against its skull. She didn't answer the knight; in truth, she didn't know what to say.

"So," War said, snapping the reins. Her horse began to walk in a slow circle around Lisa and Midnight, its hooves clanging on the pavement like death knells. Lisa shrank against Midnight, wishing she could be as brave as her own steed, trying not to imagine the red horse's teeth sinking into her arm. War said, "You're the one he picked. Can't imagine why. You've got no backbone to you."

Lisa wanted to run and hide.

"Look at you. You're just a child—practically a mouse." War let out a sound that was half laugh and half snort, and she shook her helmeted head as if in disbelief. "Well, Mouse, either you'll last or you won't. Makes no matter to me. But if I were a betting sort of person, I know where I'd put my money down."

Lisa swallowed, remembering what Death had said about War killing her. Looking at this woman, this knight with her biting horse and her brandished sword, Lisa could easily believe it. War wouldn't just kill her—she'd turn her death into an art form.

"So," War said. "Rules."

Lisa blinked in surprise. "What?"

"Rules," War repeated, her horse continuing its slow, threatening circle around Lisa and Midnight. "First rule: bring chaos. I see you're off to a decent start," she said, motioning with her sword to the restaurant behind Lisa, with its crowd of angry and wounded people and the gathering of police and news crews and ambulances. "But you'll have to do better than that, Mouse."

Lisa stammered, "Better?"

"We're the harbingers of the Apocalypse. We don't waste our time with restaurants. Think big—arenas, airports, cities," War said, her eyes glittering within her helmet's eye slots.

Dumbstruck, Lisa nodded.

"Second rule: Famine is a precursor to War. *That* means," she said, pointing the huge sword at Lisa, "you don't get in my way. You take people's food away, get them upset enough to fight. That's where *I* come in. And once I'm there, you let me do my job."

The red horse, Lisa noticed, was foaming at the mouth. "Your job," Lisa repeated, staring at the rabid creature and feeling rather faint.

"You don't want to step on my toes, girl, or I'll cut off your feet."

Eyes wide, Lisa stared at War.

"You keep the rules in mind, Mouse, especially the second, and we'll get along fine." The armor-clad woman yanked the reins, and the red steed ground to a halt, throwing its head back as if in pain or anger. "Otherwise, you'll end up just like your predecessor."

Despite herself, Lisa asked, "What happened to the last Famine?"

War chuckled, a dark and deadly sound, like the scrape of swords clearing their sheaths. "I ate the last Famine for lunch."

If she hadn't been leaning against Midnight, Lisa's legs would have given out. And she was certain that if she fainted, the red horse would trample her. *Don't pass out, don't pass out, don't pass out . . .*

War jerked the reins back, and the red horse reared onto its hind legs with a defiant scream. "You mind your betters and remember the rules," War shouted, brandishing her sword, "or I'll cut you down where you stand!"

The red steed leapt forward, and Lisa threw herself down with a shriek as the horse sailed over her, bearing its rider forward into the crowd outside the restaurant.

Panting on the ground, Lisa turned to see what happened. The people didn't react to War's presence directly as the warrior woman and her horse walked among them, her sword pointed at them. But after a minute of her attention, four fights broke out within the crowd, all of them loud and violent. Screams rent the air, punctuated with fleshy thuds and barked obscenities. All of it was captured on camera, much to the titillation of news viewers later that evening.

Lisa gripped Midnight's mane, sweating and terrified. "Take me home," she whispered to the horse. "Please."

The horse knelt, and Lisa managed to pull herself onto its back. As soon as she wrapped her fingers around the black mane, Midnight took off in a gallop, and they were gone.

░░░░░

Lisa didn't open her eyes again until Midnight halted. Even then, she waited for a silent count of ten before she took a deep breath and opened her eyes, half convinced that she'd be anywhere but home.

So it was with a huge sense of relief that she found herself back in the garden outside her house. It was still nighttime, the rhododendron bush was still noticeably barren in patches, and Death was still there, playing a guitar and singing.

Out of everything that had happened to her over the course of the day, hearing Death sing "Come as You Are" was by far the weirdest.

When he was done, he looked over at her. His face was flushed with pleasure, and his smile was warm and delightful. "I know," he said, "I should limit myself to dirges. But man, Nirvana just rocks my world."

Lisa, fumbling, said, "You sing beautifully."

"Thanks, but that's not really true. All I can do is echo the creations of others."

"Um . . . what?"

"That wasn't me playing or singing. That was Kurt Cobain."

She blinked, trying to make sense of his words. "But he's dead."

Death grinned, tapped his nose, and pointed to her. "Got it in one. So how'd it go?"

For a moment, Lisa thought he was still talking about his channeling a dead singer. Then her brain caught up and she realized Death was asking how her first outing as Famine had gone.

Flashes of memory, quicker than thought came to her . . .

Soaring in the skies; her heart bleeding with the tortured land; her stomach roiling from the human waste and apathy; a vision filled with blackness and the smell of ash; a little girl's whimpers as she is loaded into an ambulance; the sour tang of fear as a mountainous woman promises to destroy her . .

Lisa shuddered. "It was awful."

"Don't be so hard on yourself. I'm sure you did fine."

She rubbed her arms, remembering the taste of foods she'd never eaten coating her tongue, sliding down her throat as she'd turned everything to ash. God, she'd have to exercise all night just to try to work off some of the guilt she felt—and not just for foods eaten and uneaten, but for her contribution to all the violence she'd left in her wake.

Her eyes widened. *Oh no.*

Death had interrupted her workout before. She still had to burn off her dinner.

Panicked, she slid off her horse. As she tottered for balance, her mind had already focused on what she had to do next: race into the house and fly down to the basement, where she'd once again throw herself into the ritual of stationary biking. She had to work it off. She couldn't stand to be this fat.

Death said, "If it helps, horseback riding is wonderful exercise."

That stopped her. Of course, Death was right. Why, she and Midnight had traveled far . . .

"To the other side of the world," Death supplied. "Hours of travel. Each way. All in moments, of course. Time bends for creatures like us. But that doesn't change the amount of energy required."

She stared at Death, rubbing her arms to ward off the chill. "So I don't have to climb on the bike now?" Her voice was small, and so very hopeful.

"I'd say you were all set for the night." Death cocked his head, his long hair falling into his eyes. "What you really need is to get some sleep."

Lisa was going to argue the point; she was far too keyed up to even think of crawling into bed. But her words were stolen by a jaw-cracking yawn. She leaned heavily against the horse as her energy ebbed.

She turned to look at the black horse, whose breath plumed from its broad nostrils. It wasn't just her; it really was cold outside. The thought cheered her somewhat: she wasn't alone. "What about Midnight?" she asked, her words sounding fuzzy and muddled.

"Your steed will be fine. And waiting for your next ride."

"I don't have to groom it? Feed it?" Didn't she read somewhere that horses were supposed to be rubbed down after a ride?

"Our steeds are unlike mortal horses. They aren't troubled with the trappings of the living." Death paused. "Although I'd be remiss if I didn't tell you that your horse has a fondness for pralines."

A smile flitted across her lips. "Maybe I can get you some tomorrow," she said to Midnight.

The horse's ears flickered. Lisa thought Midnight was smiling.

"And no one will see it?"

"It's invisible to human eyes. Do not fear for your steed, Famine. It's been around far longer than you. It can take care of itself."

The horse cast a long, reproachful look at Death.

"Hey," Death said cheerfully, "don't look at me like that. It's true."

The horse snorted, then rubbed its muzzle in Lisa's hand.

She let out a delighted laugh. "Okay," she said, stroking the horse's nose and its neck, then patting its back. After a moment, she turned to face Death. "I met War."

The Pale Rider's face froze. Softly he said, "Did you now?"

"Yeah."

Death watched her, his expression unfathomable. "And what did you think of War?"

Lisa shivered, and this time it had nothing to do with her being cold. "She scares me."

Death nodded. "That's good."

"You scare me, too."

His eyes twinkled. "That's also good."

"I don't want to do this," she said, feeling miserable and tired and so very lost. All those people she'd hurt . . . and God help her, she was still hungry. She whispered, "Please don't make me be Famine again."

Death smiled at her—such a heartbreakingly sad smile— and said, "I can't make you be anything, Lisabeth Lewis. Only you can change what you choose to be."

Lisa looked down at her feet, wishing she were anyone other than herself.

"You'll do better after some sleep," Death said. " 'And flights of angels sing thee to thy rest.' "

Biting back a sob, she lifted her head to bid Death a good night, but the Pale Rider had disappeared.

CHAPTER 9

Lisa woke up the next morning with a spike twisting through her guts.

She curled in on herself, desperate for the pain to stop. It felt as if someone had poured cement down her throat while she'd slept—her stomach felt huge, distended, and so horribly full. Last year, she'd seen a horror movie with James and Suzanne, something about an alien that burst out of people's stomachs. She felt like that: something was trying to claw its way out of her belly, and it was taking her intestines with it.

Her head pounding, her mouth dry, she had one thought: she had to get it out.

Stumbling out of bed, she fought a wave of dizziness and staggered to the bathroom. Inside, she yanked down her pajama bottoms and her panties and squatted over the toilet.

And for the next hour, she slowly worked her way through an excruciating bowel movement, intermittently praying to God to ease the pain and swearing that she'd ask Tammy about laxatives. Tammy knew all about that sort of thing.

When Lisa was done, she flushed three times and scrubbed her hands until her fingers were shriveled prunes. Then she took one of her mother's witch hazel wipes and swabbed her seat to make sure she'd thoroughly cleaned herself. Then she flushed the pad and washed her hands again. She was sweating, but that didn't bother her; maybe she was losing water weight.

Every little bit helped. She was still dizzy, but that didn't bother her, either.

Because it was time for the morning ritual.

Lisa stripped off her flannel pajamas—first her pants, then her top. Then she folded and set the clothing on the fuzzy pink toilet seat cover. Next came her underwear, also folded and carefully placed on her pajamas. Last came her socks. She was shaking a little, so it took her longer than usual, and she nearly fell when she tugged off her right sock. Her balance was off this morning.

That didn't matter. She took a deep breath, and then submitted herself for judgment.

She stared at the full-length mirror on the back of the bathroom door, her gaze critical. She ignored her sallow skin, her sunken eyes—she hadn't slept well last night—and focused on her body. And she despaired.

You're fat, the Thin voice lamented, as it had the morning before, as it had ever since Lisa first heard the voice speaking to her. *You're so fat.*

Lisa agreed. She touched herself, running her hands over her shoulders, her waist, her hips; she sucked in her stomach and imagined what she'd look like ten pounds thinner, fifteen pounds thinner. The Thin voice suggested which foods she should cut to help make that happen.

Lisa listened. Staring at her reflection, she decided on her meal plan for the day.

And then she pulled the scale away from the wall and positioned it just so on the tile floor of the bathroom: the spot that gave her the most accurate weight reading, which she'd learned through major trial and error. Once it was in the right place on the floor, Lisa said a brief prayer. Then she stepped on the scale.

And she did it again, to make sure the number was correct.

And she did it a third time, because three times was the charm.

Feeling a hint of elation—a tenth of a pound thinner than yesterday morning!—Lisa set the scale back to its proper resting spot. But as she slipped on her panties, she caught her reflection again, and her happiness shriveled as she understood just how much further she had to go. She couldn't tell you how she'd know when she'd finally achieved her goal; in truth, she didn't know. But what she felt with all of her soul was that until she was thin, she would never be happy.

When she was thin, everything would be perfect.

Lisa cried as she put on her pajamas. By the time she'd once again covered her feet with her thick socks (better for her circulation, she'd read somewhere, and sometimes she didn't feel as cold when her feet were warm), her tears had stopped.

God, she was so tired.

She gingerly walked back to her bedroom and was dismayed to see that she had slept in; it was nearly ten o'clock. She knew she should throw on her workout clothes and climb on the bike, even before she had her first glass of water. But she was too exhausted. She'd had such odd, vivid dreams last night, something about horses and scorched food. And dying. Or maybe about death.

And scales. She remembered dreaming about scales. She let out a bitter laugh. That, at least, made sense; she couldn't remember a time lately when she wasn't thinking about her weight, or about how she needed to be thin.

Even this drained and weak, she needed to exercise. But after her bout with constipation, the last thing she wanted to do was sit on a bike seat (or any seat) for any length of time. And she was so shaky, the simple act of walking was leaving her lightheaded; there was no way she could push herself to try jogging.

Later, she decided. She'd double her evening workout on the bike to make up for the lost morning exercise time. The Thin voice, perhaps mollified by her (slight) weight loss, agreed with Lisa's decision.

Lisa pulled on her white terry cloth robe and tied the belt, cinching it tight, to help her feel thin. Yawning, she headed toward the stairs. She moved like an old woman, but that was because she was tired and sore. She'd been sick last night; she remembered throwing up at Joe's Diner. Yes, she'd had some sort of stomach bug. Poor James had to take her home early. Frowning, she tried to remember whether they'd had a fight last night. Maybe that had been the night before.

It all blurred. Everything blurred lately. Sometimes, it was so hard to think.

Lisa sighed. She needed something hot to warm her. Some tea; yes, that would do—hot caffeinated tea, no sugar or milk, of course. But she was feeling a bit evil; she'd treat herself to one of her mother's expensive brands. As long as she moved the packets around in the box to make it look as if she hadn't taken anything, her mom wouldn't notice. Appearance was everything; that was one lesson Sandy Lewis had taught her daughter well.

Downstairs, Lisa found her father in the kitchen, seated at the table. He was dressed for work, which told Lisa that even though it was Sunday, he'd be stopping by the office. He did that sometimes. The Sunday paper was spread out before him, divided into various sections. He'd left the comics for her, as always, on her usual seat. She hadn't actually been interested in the comics section in years, but her dad never noticed that, just like he'd never noticed that Lisa actually despised all the pink in her bedroom. But Lisa didn't blame him; between working so hard at the office and having to deal with her mother, Simon Lewis had enough on his plate without keeping track of all Lisa's whimsies.

He looked up from the crossword puzzle when she shuffled in. "Good morning, Princess! You slept in today." His brow furrowed as he regarded her. "How're you feeling?"

"Okay," she lied. Usually, Lisa would have been uncomfortable from her father's scrutiny, but at the moment she was just too wrung out to care. Her head was full of cotton, her stomach was still tender (albeit demanding to be fed), and her butt was sore. She took a glass from the cupboard and filled it with filtered water. It tasted flat, and it was too cold. She drank it too fast; her stomach cramped.

"You should take it easy today," her father said. "You look like you're still fighting something off. Let me get you some orange juice."

One hundred calories, the Thin voice cautioned her.

"No thanks," Lisa said, wiping her mouth. "That's a hundred calories."

Oh God, she'd said that out loud.

She rubbed her head, debated taking aspirin. Or maybe it was a caffeine headache. Yes, that was it. She made her way to the stove and grabbed the kettle. Definitely her mother's premium stash this morning.

"Sweetheart," her father chided, "everyone knows that orange juice is healthy. It's full of vitamin C."

"I'd rather eat the five oranges it takes to make one glass of juice than drink the juice," she said, more harshly than she'd intended. "And *everyone* doesn't know shit." She was sick to death of what *everyone* knew.

"Lisa," her father said, shocked.

She relented, rubbing her forehead. "Sorry. I'm just a little grumpy this morning." She tried to smile, and she ignored how it hurt her cheeks. "I guess I'm still not feeling great."

Her father smiled back, more at ease than Lisa with making everything all right again with a smile and the right words. "It's all right, Princess. I just worry about you."

That was sweet. Lisa filled the kettle and set it on the stovetop for it to boil. Then she leaned against the counter, catching her breath.

"I think you've lost some weight," Mr. Lewis said.

A surprised smile on her face, Lisa glanced at her dad. "You think so?"

But he didn't look like he was proud of her for such an accomplishment. No, instead he was looking at her critically, his hand cupping his chin and his elbow on the table. And he was frowning. "Have a seat, Princess. I'll make you some breakfast."

Her pleasure faded, and Lisa turned back to the stove. "My stomach's a little upset. I think I'll just have some tea."

"How about a slice of toast? Something to coat your stomach?"

Eighty calories, the Thin voice warned.

Why was her dad pushing food at her? And after he'd said that she'd lost weight? Was he trying to sabotage her? The thought made her want to scream. Gritting her teeth, she said, "Maybe after some tea."

Her father thankfully said nothing as she took out a tea bag and put it into a coffee mug, but Lisa felt him watching her. It made her feel angry and mean—and so damn hungry. Yes, all she wanted to do was take out a loaf of bread and a stick of butter and eat them in huge chunks, first tearing off a hunk of bread and then gobbling the butter straight; a butter sandwich, yes, that was what she wanted, bread and butter . . .

The silence stabbed her. Glaring at her father, she snapped, *"What?"*

After long pause he answered her. "I'm worried about you," he said quietly.

"I'm fine. Just not feeling great. It's a bug," she said, "that's all."

The kettle sang. Lisa poured the boiling water into her cup and let the tea steep.

"Lisa," her father said slowly, his tone setting off warning bells. "Is everything okay?"

Lisa might have said something she would have regretted, but at that moment the phone rang. Serendipity. Weak as she was feeling, she still lunged to the wall-mounted receiver and grabbed the phone, realizing too late that it might be her mother again.

"Hey," James said. "How're you feeling?"

Warmth flowed through her chest and belly. His voice had always done that to her—made her feel special, even loved. So what did it matter that normally she asked herself what he could possibly see in her, or wondered when he'd finally wake up and realize that he'd been settling when he'd asked her out?

There wasn't a day lately when they didn't fight over something, and usually, Lisa was the one who started it. He'd break up with her; of that, she had no doubt. He deserved better than her. But right now, she was so relieved to hear his voice that she nearly sobbed from joy.

"Hi," she said, sinking into a chair. "A little better. My stomach still isn't good," she added, thinking of her bathroom excursion.

"Sorry about that. You up for me swinging by? You mentioned something about plying me with cookies, and I'd promised you chicken soup . . ."

Lisa giggled, imagining him waggling his brows. She could beg off the soup, claiming her stomach wouldn't handle it— even though the thought of sipping the hot broth made her head swimmy. No, no; she was in control. "Sure. I have to shower, and I promised Tammy I'd come over at one. Want to say eleven thirty?"

"Sure," James said, sounding forced.

Normally, Lisa would have let it go, but this morning she was prickly. "What?"

"Nothing. I'm happy to ration my time with my girlfriend."

She blew out a sigh. "That's not fair. I had plans with her before I had plans with you."

"Yeah. You just spend an awful lot of time with her lately," James said. "You sure you don't want to date her?"

Don't get mad. Don't get mad. "Do you want me to cancel my plans with her?" she asked tightly. Tammy would kill her. But . . . this was James. She had to make the offer.

It was James's turn to sigh. "No, don't do that," he said, and

Lisa let out a breath she hadn't realized she'd been holding. "I just don't know why you hang out with her so much. She can be so bitchy."

"Tammy's a friend," she said, defensive. Tammy understood her.

James backpedaled quickly, saying, "Well, anyway. Yeah, I'll swing by around eleven thirty. That's . . . what, forty minutes? Damn, I have to go get the soup."

"Hey, you don't have to—"

"Of course I do," he said with a chuckle. "You're my girlfriend, and you're under the weather. Chicken soup cures everything."

Lisa smiled sadly. If only that were true. "Okay."

"I'll bring a surprise, too. Something I think you need."

Ooh. Gamely, she said, "What is it?"

Now he let out a belly laugh. "If I told you, it wouldn't be a surprise. You'll see."

They said their goodbyes, and Lisa hung up the phone, anticipation swirling in her belly. A surprise, from James?

"That sounds like it went well."

Lisa smiled sheepishly at her father. She'd forgotten he'd been sitting there; of course he'd heard everything.

"Except for the part when you argued about Tammy," Mr. Lewis added.

Lisa shrugged. "Boyfriends and best friends sometimes don't get along."

"I thought Suzanne was your best friend."

Lisa bristled. "We had a falling-out."

"Sorry to hear that." He looked it, too. Lisa wasn't surprised; her father liked Suzanne. Heck, her father liked everyone—even her mother. He said, "Maybe you'll work it out."

"Maybe," she said, not believing it. "James is coming over in a little bit. I have to go shower."

Her father laughed, waving a hand at her. "Go on. I know how long it takes women to get ready. You know, when your mother and I go anywhere, I have to tack on an extra twenty minutes of mirror-gazing time for her, to make sure every lock of hair is perfect."

His words, probably meant to be kind, stabbed Lisa even more than the gut-wrenching pain she'd woken to. She smiled blandly and said something inane, then retreated upstairs.

But before she showered, she once again looked at herself, naked, searching out all her flaws before she stepped into a steaming jet of water and tried to scour away her imperfections.

The entire time, she thought of burned food and parched earth.

||||||

Lisa heard the doorbell, and she frantically tugged the brush through her hair. More strands pulled free. Combined with what she'd cleaned out of the shower drain, she was surprised she had any hair left at all; lately, she was shedding enough to be a sheepdog in high summer. Her hair was brittle, too, so she'd gone heavy with the conditioner. That had backfired spectacularly, because now her hair was limp as a dead thing. Fueled by desperation, she gathered everything into a ponytail and yanked it tight, winding an elastic round and round.

Staring critically at her reflection, she decided she liked the way the drastic pull of her hairdo made her eyebrows seem sleek and tapered. She touched up her eyeliner as her father heartily welcomed James into the house, booming something about another lifetime of servitude.

She smiled. Men were so weird.

Lisa was lightheaded, but she assumed that was from the steaming hot shower. She'd taken her time and had done a full-leg shave, even trimmed her bikini area—not that she was planning on James and her getting physical with her dad right there in the house, yuck—and then moisturized her knees and ankles and elbows. Her skin had been patchy lately, and she did her best to even out her tone. *More water,* she decided. Water would flush out all the bad and leave her with hydrated skin. She'd have to bump up her water intake to more than a gallon a day.

Going slowly, she headed out of her bedroom, only a little wobbly in her low-heeled boots. For some reason, she had Nirvana in her head, and she hummed the opening to "Come As You Are" as she made her way down the stairs.

She stopped short as she saw who was with James and her father by the front door.

"Hi, Leese," Suzanne said.

CHAPTER 10

"What is *she* doing here?" Lisa said to James, pointedly refusing to look at her former friend. How dare she show her face here, after what she'd said to Lisa last week? After what she'd accused her of?

She heard it again in her mind, Suzanne's words shaky and broken with tears: *"You're anorexic, Lisa."*

Anorexic. Please. That was just stupid and insulting. Lisa wasn't anorexic.

You're too fat to be anorexic, the Thin voice sighed.

Suzanne said, "Leese, I want us to talk."

Despite herself, Lisa glared at Suzanne. Her former friend looked small as she stood in the doorway, bundled against the cold in an oversize muffler. *Good,* Lisa thought. *She should be cold. What she said to me was cold.*

"Can I please come in?" Suzanne asked.

"No."

"Of course you can," Mr. Lewis said brightly, casting a look at his daughter. "Come on—it's cold out there." He ushered Suzanne inside, and the girl stood in the foyer next to James, looking both nervous and determined.

Lisa narrowed her eyes. "Dad . . ."

"She wants to talk," her father said to her, sounding curt and not at all like the perfect dad he usually was. "Surely, after being friends since you were six, the least you can do is listen."

Furious, Lisa stood mute. How could her father pick Suzanne over her? Did they put him up to this? Had James spoken with her dad about doing this?

Oh God. What else had James been doing behind her back?

"Thanks, Mr. Lewis," Suzanne said.

They stood there, her father and James and Suzanne in the foyer and Lisa on the stairs, none of them saying anything. Lisa had never felt so betrayed, so completely lost. She hated them all, felt that hatred sear her, scar her; she wanted to burn them all into ash, as she'd done with the food in her dream; scorch them off the face of the earth.

Creepers of shadow inched along her vision, and she thought she was going to black out.

Suck them dry, the Thin voice urged. *They deserve it.* Only now it wasn't the Thin voice, no, but rather the voice from her dream—a large woman in armor, brandishing a sword. *Cut them down where they stand.*

Lisa's fists trembled.

"Well," her father said. The sound of his voice snapped Lisa out of the black place, and she blinked furiously, clearing her vision. Her father, unaware of how close his daughter had come to hurting him and the others, kept talking. "I know you girls have been fighting. It's time for you to move past that. Friends forgive each other," he said, looking right at Lisa.

She bit back the hateful things she wanted to spew at her father.

"I know you'll do the right thing," he said to her. "I'll leave you alone to work things out."

Of course, Lisa thought bitterly. Her father was going to run away, leave her defenseless while her boyfriend and former best friend attacked her.

Lisa was alone. She would always be alone.

She wanted to die.

"I have to head to the office for a while," Mr. Lewis said, as if Lisa actually cared what his excuse was. He grabbed his coat from the closet and walked over to the stairs to where Lisa stood. "I'll see you later, Princess." He kissed her brow.

Lisa couldn't reply, but the confusion and horror and heartache in her eyes spoke volumes for her.

Her father sighed and stiffly patted her shoulder. "You'll work it out," he said somberly, and then he walked toward the kitchen. A moment later, Lisa heard the back door open and close. For a second, she thought she heard a horse neigh before the door shut, cutting off outside noise.

The sound—imagined, surely—gave her strength. "So," she said to James, "I guess *this* is my surprise. I would've liked another pair of earrings much better."

"Leese, come on," he said, his hands out in an appeal. "Give Suzie a chance."

"To do what? Insult me again?"

"Lisa," Suzanne said, "I never meant—"

"I wasn't talking to *you*," Lisa spat. "I have nothing to say to *you*."

Suzanne cringed.

"Leese," James said imploringly, "this isn't like you. Friends give each other a chance."

Her head was spinning, and her stomach roiled, bubbling with venom. Not like her? Well, maybe she was tired of always being a doormat. She sneered, "Yeah? Well, you can tell *her* that friends don't hurt each other. Friends don't call each other horrible names."

James's gaze was hard, though his voice was soft: a contradiction of affection. "Friends tell each other the truth."

"You didn't hear what she'd called me," she snarled. "Or what she'd said about me."

"Yes, I did. She told me. She thinks you're anorexic," James said, stunning Lisa into silence. But nothing could have prepared her for the rest of what he had to say. "And I agree with her."

The words hit Lisa like a blow, and she sat down hard on the stairs.

James agreed with Suzanne? The world officially made no sense anymore. Her boyfriend was supposed to be supportive; he was supposed to have her back. A mewling sound escaped her mouth—not a cry, not a whine, but caught somewhere in between. Her breath strangled in her throat and her face burned. For the first time in who knew how long, Lisabeth Lewis didn't feel hungry.

She felt nothing at all, except a cold, raw rage simmering in her belly.

"Can we go inside?" James asked. "Sit on the sofa, maybe?"

"No. No, I think you can stay right where you are." Lisa's voice was faint, which was so odd, considering she wanted to scream at the top of her lungs. But she just didn't have the energy. No screaming. No pitching a fit.

No trust. No nothing.

James thought she was anorexic. What a joke. If she were anorexic, she'd actually be thin, and then she wouldn't have to worry about eating all the time. She let out a laugh, one that scraped her throat and bled on her tongue.

"Leese," Suzanne said, her hands fluttering like nervous birds, "I didn't mean to hurt your feelings. But I'm worried about you."

"So am I," James said.

They were worried about her? Yeah, right. Listen to them scolding her, accusing her. Turning her own father against her. "You talked about me behind my back." Her voice was flat and so very cold.

"You're not eating," Suzanne said.

"Of course I am."

"You're exercising all the time."

"No I'm not," Lisa said. God knew, she hadn't done anything today.

"You're vomiting in the bathroom," James said.

Lisa balled her hands into fists. "It was one time, and I was sick." She wanted to throw her head back and scream, but all that came out was her queer, toneless voice, as if she were a robot. It was as if James's accusation had sucked all the life out of her.

He didn't understand. No one understood, except maybe Tammy, a little.

"You're not acting like *you*, Lisa," Suzanne said. "We think you need help."

Lisa smiled wanly. "Do you now?" If Tammy were here, she'd laugh her head off before giving James and Suzanne both a piece of her mind. Tammy would be strong and confident.

Unlike Lisa, who could only sit there and play dead.

Suzanne swallowed and bit her lip. James, though, met her gaze without flinching. "We do, Leese. We think you need to go to your doctor and get help."

"Uh-huh."

"Talk to someone," Suzanne said, wringing her hands. "You know, a professional."

Oh yes. That was exactly what Lisa wanted: to tell a stranger her most intimate thoughts. She croaked out a laugh, and tears spilled down her sallow cheeks.

James knelt down before her and took her hand. "Lisa, will you please listen to us?"

Us. James and Suzanne and her father. Probably her mother, too. All of them had turned against her.

She pulled her hand away. "Get out of my house."

James stayed frozen in a parody of proposal. Suzanne looked as if she'd been kicked in the stomach—ill and green and so desperately unhappy.

Lisa lurched to her feet. The room spun drunkenly, and she closed her eyes to find her balance.

Balance, Death whispered—a memory or a promise, Lisa couldn't tell.

It hadn't been a dream, she realized, her eyes snapping open. Death really had come to her and made her Famine. The horse she'd heard was hers, her steed.

Her eyes shone. Yes. She'd find Death. He understood her.

She pushed past James, ignored his protest and Suzanne's cries as she ran to the kitchen, her boots clacking against the linoleum. She yanked open the back door and let out a cry of relief as she saw her steed, black as the darkest night, black as death (even though Death rode a pale horse and not a black one), waiting for her in the garden. Her mother's bushes were noticeably bare.

"Midnight, you're real," she said, relieved.

The horse snorted and flicked its ears. Then it knelt in the grass and nodded to its mistress.

Laughing like a madwoman, Lisabeth Lewis launched herself on the black horse's back and tangled her fingers in its mane. "Death," she said to her steed. "Take me to Death."

The horse snorted again, then leapt into the sky.

On its back, Lisa pretended she didn't hear James and Suzanne calling to her, begging her to come back.

CHAPTER 11

They galloped across the skies, the world streaking beneath them in colorful waves that rippled when Lisa glanced down. Or maybe her tears distorted what she saw. It didn't matter. Her problems were far away, a lifetime away. They rode the path of Famine, and for a time, Lisa didn't think of herself. Instead she lost herself to the thrill of the ride—the way her hair whipped back, the feeling of the horse beneath her. On Midnight's back, Lisa was free.

Freedom, of course, came with a price. And that payment came due as they slowed over a mountainous terrain, passing over verdant jungle: dew-kissed emeralds and lush jades; darkling peridots and sunny chartreuses. Everywhere, it seemed, were green fields, a farmer's delight. The vegetation spoke of life and health, and it lightened Lisa's heart.

But then they swooped low, and she saw that the crops were riddled with desiccated stalks and brown husks, tantalizingly green at their tips but rotted at their bases. Entire fields of maize and paddy had been destroyed before they even had a chance to ripen. Ruined before maturity.

Starved.

Lisa swallowed thickly as she peered at the crops. And her mouth twisted in disgust from the gray-brown bodies that undulated within all the green like a river of cancer. Rats— thousands of them; hundreds of thousands. They devoured the living smorgasbord in an almost lazy way—scavengers, even when sated, never ceased in their hunger for more.

Midnight touched down at the outskirts of a dusty village littered with shacks. Fences separated the fields from the washed-out town, and Lisa realized they were trying to keep the rats out of the crops. It was as fruitless as the trees on the mountain; fences and traps couldn't contain such a plague. Looming poles dangled vermin with snapped necks, but where ten rats were caught, thousands more roamed free.

Free, like her. The thought made her cringe in her seat.

On Midnight's back, Lisa toured the land. She took in the desolate huts, the dilapidated structures that listed in the wind. She watched brown-skinned farmers, barefoot and thin, as they tossed rats into debris piles of shredded wood and dead crops. Men with sinewy arms hoisted line after line of dead rodents, but it did little good. Their crops were ruined, sacrificed to the vermin god.

And as the scavengers feasted in the fields, the villagers starved. Lisa saw mothers ignoring their own raking hunger pangs as they fed their emaciated children, babies with their stomachs bloated and their limbs like twigs. She saw fathers toiling to catch rats or to hunt in the neighboring jungles for food. Even the livestock—pigs and cows and chickens—were scrawny from hunger, their ribs all too clear beneath their bodies as the animals rooted in the dirt. In one large hut, dozens of men and women gathered by cook pots, sharing the little food they had: yams and bananas and leaves from the jungles around the village.

And rats, of course. The villagers ate the very creatures that were forcing them closer to mass starvation.

Lisa could tell what was in the cook pots, even as she could tell the rats from the dirt. She was Famine, and she felt the people's hunger like a monstrous tick burrowing under her skin. Groaning, she wrapped her arms around her stomach. This wasn't incessant appetite or some internal appeal to be fed that she could ignore. This was a tortured beast bellowing, scrabbling toward either survival or surrender.

This was unbearable.

"Why did you bring me here?" she whispered.

Midnight ignored her question and walked on, weaving between ramshackle dwellings and empty storage huts. When the horse came to a halt and knelt, Lisa breathed in a sweet odor like leaf rot and spilled honey. Deeper, though, was the putrid stench of spoiled milk in the sun.

Lisa stared at the scene before her, shocked into wide-eyed silence.

The bodies looked almost like dolls—life-size dolls of flesh stretched too tightly over skeletons. Gravediggers worked, their mouths and noses covered by dusty bandannas as their shovels winked almost merrily in the sunlight. The people watching leaned against one another for support, or out of exhaustion, or maybe because they just couldn't stand upright any longer. One woman sat at the edge of the pit, her tears gleaming like jewels, her sobs silent. On her lap was a doll of a child, its eyes closed.

Numb, Lisa counted the bodies. Six people dead, and five of them were children. Babies. She had asked her steed to take her to Death, and it had—but not the death she'd wished for.

Wishes and horses, she thought, feeling hollow and sad and mad and sick. Her stomach lurched. Lisa clamped a hand to her mouth and told herself not to vomit.

"You get used to the stench of death," a man said, "but the smell never really leaves you."

Swallowing the bile that had risen in her throat, she pivoted to face a tall man seated on a white horse. Dust hovered around him like a nimbus, but the white of his coat—and of his horse—remained immaculate, untouched.

She stared at him, at his horse, at the silver crown that sparkled on the man's brow, bright against his greasy black hair. His pockmarked face was waxy, his eyes rheumy. Cold sores peppered his mouth like lipsticked kisses.

Yuck.

She focused on the scarred man, even as the smell of death teased her like perfume dancing on a breeze. "You're a Horseman," she said, her voice tremulous from almost vomiting— and, honestly, from being so close to a man who looked so nasty.

His smile was a perfunctory flash. "Pestilence."

Remembering her encounter with War, and how she'd nearly gotten her hand bitten off, Lisa didn't offer to shake hands. Besides, she really didn't want to touch him. She wondered if he had leprosy.

"Of course I do," he snapped. "I bear all diseases. It's my lot in life."

Great, another Horseman who could read her mind. Embarrassed, she bit her lip. "Sorry," she said. "I didn't mean to hurt your feelings." It occurred to her, then, that she sounded exactly like Suzanne.

"Of course you didn't. People never mean anything they say or think." He snorted, and snot flew from his nostrils.

She blushed, but the White Rider kept talking—ranting, really.

"'How are you,' they ask, and they never really want an answer. No one wants to hear about how people are slowly dying a little more every day."

Lisa, unsure of what to say, held her tongue.

"People are hypocrites," Pestilence said. "It sickens me."

"Um." What did one say to someone like him? "Are you here because they're sick?"

"Of course." He looked down his nose at her. "Much as you're here because they're starving. Famine and Pestilence work well together. We always have."

"Oh?" She pasted a smile on her face to hide her disgust.

"Look at these villagers," he said, motioning with a white-gloved hand. "Normally self-sufficient, they had once again planned on their crops to support themselves. But then the bamboo flowered. Life," he said with a smirk. "Life begets all evils of the world."

Oh boy. Lisa's smile slipped. "Bamboo flowers?" She'd thought bamboo was a reed. Her mother had a collection of bamboo baskets.

"And with the flowers came the rats."

Lisa shuddered.

"And the rats, once here, feasted on bamboo, on maize, on all manner of crops. Entire fields, destroyed overnight." His pink-rimmed eyes glistened either with disease or with tears. "With no crops, the people gather what they can. Yams, dug out in the jungle. Bananas, too, when they're lucky. Roots and leaves."

"And rats," Lisa whispered.

"And rats," he agreed. "And that's when they're fortunate enough to have food to go around. When they don't, they starve."

"How about a slice of toast?" her father had asked her just this morning. And she'd said no, because the Thin voice had warned her that the toast was eighty calories. Once again, Lisa thought she would vomit.

"Children die soonest," Pestilence said, "as do the elderly and the sick. Even if they don't die of hunger, they suffer from diarrhea and gastritis, which in this place leads to death. With no crops to sell, there is no money to buy mosquito netting, and so at night their bodies are a feast for mosquitoes. And in the morning they awaken with malaria. Yes," he said, "Famine and Pestilence have always worked well together. And we pave the way for Death. We are Death's harbingers."

Her head spinning from the White Rider's words, Lisa said, "And War is Death's handmaiden."

"War," Pestilence said, sneering. He spat noisily, and where his spittle landed, the ground sizzled. "War sees this all as a glorious battle."

"It's . . . not?"

He shot her a pitying look. "A horseman is one who rides a horse. There's nothing in the description that calls us to arms."

"Then . . ." She looked at the burial, then back at the White Rider. "Did you cause the sickness here?"

He snorted. "Did you cause the famine?"

"Of course not," she said, shocked.

"Like you, I was drawn here. We don't cause the ills of the world, little Famine."

"Then . . . what are we supposed to do?"

"Do?" A horrific smile oozed along his face. "A thousand rats destroyed this village practically overnight. The Great Pestilence wiped out more than seventy-five million people in the fourteenth century. Smallpox killed more than three hundred million people in the twentieth century." He paused, searching her face. "What makes you think those numbers couldn't have been higher?"

She blinked. "What?"

"Do you have any idea how easy it would be for a plague to annihilate all of humanity?" he said drolly. "Especially these days, with scientists mucking about in their labs, all those diseases lined up like toy soldiers?"

She could picture it all too easily.

"I am quite busy keeping things in check, thank you very much." Pestilence brushed at his collar, as if to flick away the dusty aura surrounding him. "You'd think I sit around, whiling away my time eating chocolates."

Hershey's Kisses, the Thin voice said. *Twenty-five calories.*

Shut up, Lisa scolded.

Amazingly, the Thin voice fell silent. Lisa had never stood up to it before.

"Unlike War," Pestilence said with a sneer, "my duty is both local and global. Disease is rampant, pandemic. The Spanish flu killed twenty million people around the world. More than thirty-three million people have AIDS today."

Lisa's head swam as she tried to understand his words. "So you . . . help people?"

"Well, if everyone dies, I'd be out a job, wouldn't I?"

She waved a hand at the villagers. "So help them! Cure them!"

His liquid gaze locked on to hers, and she thought he was

trying to tell her something silently, implore her to action or to understanding.

"You know," he finally said, "you and I are very much alike."

The very notion nauseated her.

"Famine attacks people from without, destroying their food sources. Pestilence attacks from within, destroying their bodies. But whether from without or within, we achieve the same result. We destroy."

"What are you saying?"

"We are the Horsemen of the Apocalypse, little Famine. We don't cure people. We destroy. That's all we've ever done."

Lisa turned away from him. She didn't want him to see her cry. Slowly, the villagers buried their dead.

"As early as 200 B.C.," Pestilence said, "people experimented with vaccination. The Chinese, the Indians, the Turks; they all dabbled. Then came Edward Jenner, with his theory of milkmaids and cowpox. Humans have gone from gifting natives with smallpox blankets to eradicating smallpox completely. You see? People can fight using disease. Or they can inject themselves with it to cure themselves. But whichever path they choose, they first must understand disease intimately."

Lisa frowned.

"The first thing you must do, little Famine, is understand hunger."

She faced him, holding her chin high. "I think I already do."

He inclined his head in acknowledgment. "Indeed."

"So you're saying I don't have to hurt people?" she asked, her words hesitant. "I can help them? Somehow?"

He smiled again, twisting his face into a parody of mirth. "As I said, you and I are very much alike."

She looked down at her hands, remembered what she'd done at the restaurant just yesterday, at Joe's Diner the night before. "But how?"

"That you'll discover as you walk your path. Or," he said, "as you ride. We are Horsemen, after all."

"War said that my purpose was to get people to fight about food, and then she'd do the rest."

"Yes, well, War has been known to twist things her own way. She's the politician out of the four of us."

Lisa looked up at Pestilence on his white horse, like some mockery of a knight who'd come to save her. "What does that make you?"

"The philanthropist," he said, tipping an imaginary hat. With that, the White Rider nudged his steed, and both man and horse disappeared in a cloud of dust.

Lisa stayed until all six bodies were in the ground. When the last shovelful of dirt filled the pit, she quietly said a prayer for the dead. She wasn't a religious girl, but clearly there were powers out there; she and the other Horsemen were proof of that.

"God," she said somberly, "their deaths were stupid. Please welcome their souls to heaven, because they deserve better than what they got here." After a moment, she added, "And if you don't mind, help me figure out my path, like Pestilence said. Um, please. Because as messed up as I am, I don't want to mess up other people. Thank you. Amen."

As she and Midnight turned to leave, she thought she heard a familiar voice say, "Go thee out unto the world."

But when she looked around for Death's familiar face, she was alone.

CHAPTER 12

The black horse set Famine down outside the human's house, as she'd requested. The steed had neighed its opinion—there were many other places that beckoned to them, areas ripe with abundance, where the horn of plenty was constantly sucked dry by gluttons—but even so, the horse did as its mistress had asked. It was loyal, even when its rider was foolish.

Really, a human's *house?* Why waste time with a bare handful of people when the entire world waited for Famine's touch? The horse snorted. Even after its millennia of existence, it would never, ever understand people.

It knelt so that Famine could dismount. After she did so, she patted its neck and murmured thanks as sweet to its ears as pralines to its tongue. Its previous rider had never been so considerate. Maybe it was because this rider was still young—and still human. Whatever the reason for the affection, the steed enjoyed Famine's attention.

The horse stood guard until its mistress entered the abode. Then it scanned the landscaped bushes, and its ears quivered when it spied a bright array of chrysanthemums. It trotted over to the autumn flowers and began to snack.

Not pralines, no. But still quite tasty.

Lisa should have known things would go sour when Tammy overreacted to Lisa's not bringing any of her homemade cookies.

"You promised," Tammy grumbled. "You said so yesterday, so I didn't go shopping today." *Shopping* was code for Tammy scouring the pantry, raiding it for store-brand cookies and packaged cakes and other sweets, for chocolate bars and pretzels and potato chips. Lisa knew that Tammy never actually went to the store to supply her binges; why should she, when her mother and sister—obese, the two of them—were all too happy to fill the shelves to capacity with junk food?

But like Lisa, Tammy had her rituals. And Lisa had blown it for her.

"I'm sorry," Lisa said again as Tammy searched the shelves for the foods she needed for binging. As always, Tammy was in control; even in the grip of her desire to stuff herself to the bursting point, she would only do so with specific foods. It was completely unlike what Lisa did whenever she would inevitably cave and eat (and eat and eat; whenever she gave in, it was as if her stomach were a bottomless pit). During those bleak times, Lisa went with whatever food had seduced her—a jar of peanut butter, a loaf of potato bread, a bag of chocolates. Lisa had no control. Tammy, however, had a particular routine. Even now, pissed off as all get out, she exuded confidence, determination.

"Uh-huh." Tammy slammed cabinet doors, stormed through the kitchen, spewing venom as if to prepare herself for spewing food. "No warning, no prep time. And my mom will be home in ninety minutes."

Mortified, Lisa said again, "Sorry."

"It was totally thoughtless of you." Tammy glared at Lisa. "What, did your guy come over and distract you?"

"Something like that," Lisa muttered.

"Next time, don't make promises if you're not going to keep them."

Abashed, Lisa watched Tammy as the girl pulled out various foods from various places. Normally, she would have been horrified by the thought of letting Tammy down. But even though Lisa felt bad about forgetting her promise, there were other things occupying her mind. She was still wounded from James and Suzanne working together to attack her, and still very uneasy from her meeting with Pestilence.

And she smelled death *everywhere*. It was as if the odor had permeated her skin. She'd tried scrubbing her hands when she'd first arrived at Tammy's place, but the smell lingered, subtle, insidious—a reminder that life meant death, that satisfaction was fleeting.

Balance, Death had told her. Like the Scales she had . . . somewhere. Could she summon them right now? Would Tammy even see them? What would happen if Tammy touched them?

Worse, what if Lisa brandished her symbol of office . . . and used that power against her friend, the way she nearly had against her father and the others? The way she had yesterday at a restaurant in another part of the world?

What if War showed up?

Troubled, Lisa said, "Maybe I should go."

Tammy stiffened, then turned to face her. "Hey, look. I'm sorry. I know, I'm bitchy today." She offered Lisa a sheepish smile. "It's that time of the month, you know? My stomach's all wonky."

Of course, that has nothing to do with all of the binging and purging.

Lisa bit down on that thought, shoved it away. What on earth was wrong with her? It wasn't like her to judge Tammy. She did her best to always be considerate. "Sure," she said, giving Tammy a smile in return. "Look, if you want, I can head back, pick up the cookies . . ."

"No, it's all right. I found where Mom keeps the good ones." Grinning, she held up a package of cookies. "Not like freshly baked, but hey, beggars and choosers."

It took her almost twenty minutes, but finally Tammy made her selections while Lisa watched. The girls chatted lightheartedly, but it was all audible flotsam. Tammy's concentration was on choosing foods. Lisa was just filling the silence.

Tammy scooped all of the foods she'd picked into a plastic bag, and then the girls headed into Tammy's bedroom. Lisa, familiar with the routine, shut the door behind them, even though they had the house to themselves. "You never know when someone's coming around," Tammy liked to say.

On Tammy's bed—full-size, unlike Lisa's twin, and not a hint of pink to be found—Lisa watched as her friend arranged her junk food in a row near the pillows: potato chips, cupcakes, chocolate bar, cookies, frosting. Tammy put a carton of milk on the floor.

"Skim milk," Lisa noted.

"Mom's out of the two percent," Tammy replied, shrugging. She turned on her television and flicked through the channels until she settled on one particular show that Lisa didn't recognize. Onscreen, a handsome flavor of the day made insipid remarks to a laugh track. Satisfied, Tammy settled down by the head of the bed and dug into her stash, ripping open a bag of chips.

By the foot of the bed, Lisa watched Tammy from the corner of her eye. Fascinated by the culinary train wreck, Lisa watched her friend peripherally, quietly enjoying how the Thin voice was utterly silent. As usual, Lisa timed Tammy's binge.

Potato chips, chased with milk. Seven minutes. Lisa wondered if Tammy tasted the food as she ate, if the skim milk made the chips taste like crunchy mashed potatoes. Every sound that Tammy made grated in Lisa's ears: the chomping, the gulping, the swallowing. It shouldn't bother her, she told herself. She watched the television screen and schooled her face to impassivity.

Next, two cupcakes. For the first piece, Tammy ate the filling and cake together. She split the second cupcake up the middle, licking the filling first and then eating the cake. More milk. Nine minutes.

On the television set, a family sat down to dinner. They argued to a backdrop of laughter. Tammy ate, and Lisa felt nauseated.

Tammy reached for a chocolate bar and removed the wrapper. She nibbled the outer ridge almost daintily, then clamped down, finishing the bar in six bites. Milk. Four minutes.

Lisa's stomach growled, saying that it, too, wanted to be stuffed. But then she thought of dead children, their bodies like broken dolls. Her stomach settled, perhaps out of respect.

Tammy ate. Cookies, now, with milk-chocolate frosting spread thickly on top. Still more milk. Sixteen minutes.

A lifetime, as the dead children went into their pit of a grave, tucked in with blankets of dirt.

Tammy pulled herself off the bed, tossing the remote control to Lisa. "Back in about twenty," Tammy announced. She staggered out, and Lisa stared at the discarded wrappers on the bed, scattered like dead leaves on the earth.

Like dead rats before a cook pot.

She heard the bathroom door shut and the lock click into place, and she shuddered. Lisabeth Lewis closed her eyes.

A moment later, Famine opened them.

Her black gaze followed Tammy into the bathroom, watched the girl gather her hair back into a ponytail and wind it into a bun at the top of her head, saw Tammy strip off her shirt and reach into the bathtub to turn on the water. The water poured out, life-giving water, its sounds filling the bathroom. Tammy removed her bra and unzipped her jeans.

Famine watched with pitiless eyes, knowing the girl didn't want to get vomit on her clothing because the smell would never come out of the shirt. With her left hand, Tammy braced herself against the porcelain toilet bowl. Her right index and middle fingers tickled the back of her throat. When she didn't retch, the girl turned on the sink faucet and gulped down water. Then she turned back to the toilet and tried again.

The water came spurting back out of her, bringing some food with it. Tammy's fingers reached down. This time, the milk came up in mottled white chunks. She gripped the bowl as she puked. When no more food came up, she rinsed her fingers off in the sink, then crouched again before the porcelain toilet.

Famine saw the spewed food floating in the bowl like drowned maggots, felt the food spraying from the girl's mouth. Tammy's nose ran freely. Her eyes watered. Her knees threatened to buckle. Famine felt all of it.

It slipped into the rhythm of routine: insert finger, vomit, rinse, repeat. Tammy flushed the toilet when the bowl was filled with more regurgitated food than water. She rinsed off her fingers and wiped her nose. Tammy knew she shouldn't have a problem with not washing her fingers until she was completely done, but she couldn't put her fingers in her mouth when they were caked with undigested food. It was too nasty.

Famine knew Tammy's thoughts; she felt Tammy's throat burn from stomach acid, her esophagus weaken closer to a rupturing point, her tooth enamel erode. Tammy, oblivious to her body's reactions, reached down, heaved. A large mass of solid food flooded out her mouth. Both of her hands grasped the bowl as her body rippled with spasms. Chips and cupcakes and chocolate splattered in the toilet. Brown globs splashed up and sprayed Tammy's face, flicking against her lashes. She flushed again, wiping her eyelids and nose.

Famine, relentless, bore witness.

It took fifteen minutes from start to finish. When Tammy was done, she sank down in the corner, knees pulled up to her chest, arms crossed over her legs. She rubbed her hands over her arms, her fingers raw from constant exposure to stomach acid. She leaned her head against the wall as her breath came in ragged pants. Tears meandered down her cheeks, and her eyes swam with misery.

Famine watched, her black eyes blazing.

Soon Tammy got up and rinsed her hands and face. She brushed her teeth and gargled with mouthwash. She shut the water from the sink and tub, and she wiped down the toilet seat. She splattered tap water onto her neck and chest, removing any stray particles that had found their way onto her skin.

She urinated. When she was done, she took off her jeans and ran her hand over her stomach, then stepped onto the scale.

Famine watched Tammy look down and sniffle, watched Tammy slowly get dressed again. She watched Tammy spray Lysol in the small room, masking the stink of sickness with the stench of canned roses. She watched Tammy slap a grin onto her face that looked sickly as she opened the bathroom door.

Famine, done watching, closed her eyes. And Lisa opened them as Tammy came back into the bedroom. Feeling scooped out and confused, Lisa stared at the TV screen, trying to focus on a mindless sitcom.

Tammy wasn't in control at all. It was an act, a *lie*. Lisa had seen that with every spray of partially digested food that had hit Tammy's face. She had felt Tammy's agony, her self-loathing, her burning desire to be thin. She was disciplined only in as much that her particular routine of food ruled her life. That wasn't control. That was surrender.

Lisa understood that all too well.

All those months ago, Tammy had made it sound as if she were sharing something important with Lisa by telling her about her binging, about her purging. And Lisa had felt as if she'd found a sister, someone who understood her own fears about being fat. But Tammy didn't understand any more than Lisa did. Lisa had seen that as Famine.

Tammy had betrayed her even worse than James and Suzanne had, and worse than her father had.

God, no one understood. She had no one to turn to.

Lisa wanted to cry, or shriek, or take a knife and cut herself until she bled dry. She hated her life. She wanted to die.

But she didn't think Death would be so kind to her this time.

"Well," Tammy said after a few minutes of strained silence, "no worries, everything came out okay."

Lisa didn't think the usual joke was funny. Cold, she rubbed her arms.

"Wow, you really are a buzzkill today," Tammy commented.

Thinking about Tammy making herself puke out of fear, imagining rats scurrying in Tammy's pantry and eating all of the food stored there, Lisa said, "Got into a fight with James." That was perfectly true, if not what was actually on her mind.

"Ooh! Dirt!" Lisa wasn't looking at Tammy, but the girl sounded as if she were salivating. The naked hunger in her voice made Lisa feel sick. Tammy demanded, "What happened?"

"I don't want to talk about it."

Three beats before Tammy sniffed, "Well fine. Way to trust your best friend."

Lisa had nothing to say.

She and Tammy stared at the television set, the air between them thick with resentment and anger and a sense of sadness, and of something lost. The bond between them, always fragile, had finally shattered.

Onscreen, a perfect television family experienced their perfect television problems. In half an hour, everything was television perfect again.

Lisa left before the credits finished rolling. If Tammy tried to stop her, Lisa was too caught up in her own bleak thoughts to notice.

CHAPTER 13

Lisa walked out of Tammy's house in a daze, her head cottony thick, her chest heavy. She hadn't grabbed a jacket when she'd fled her own house that morning, but she didn't feel cold. She was too numb to feel much of anything. Even the hunger inside of her, the hunger that defined her, had been reduced from a raging boil to a low simmer.

Those she'd held closest to her had all betrayed her trust, each and every one of them. This came on top of how for the past two days she'd been thrown into an insane situation, traveling across the world on the back of a black horse and commanded to deal in starvation—or possibly salvation, if the White Rider were to be believed. (And, admittedly, Lisa didn't believe him. If Pestilence was the philanthropist of the Horsemen, then Lisa was the cynic.)

It was just too much.

She walked past Midnight, who looked up from the chrysanthemums as she approached and then flared its nostrils as she went past. It whinnied at her, perhaps trying to snap her out of her funk. But she walked on, her feet on autopilot as she headed toward home. The steed snorted, cast a longing look at the flowers, and then followed its mistress, a black specter shadowing her like misery.

No one saw Lisa or the horse; people walked around them as if to avoid a cold spot, or suddenly crossed the street, or just an-

gled themselves to go around them. Normal people don't per-
ceive the otherworldly that hover in this world. It's a Darwinist
safety switch in the mind, something to help keep humans from
screaming at shadows. But deep in our souls, or our collective
unconsciousness, we know those things we hesitate to define are
there, walking among us. We know, even if we don't see.

Lisabeth Lewis walked on, and the steed of Famine
followed.

Maybe the horse's presence influenced the shape of Lisa's
thoughts. Even though she didn't want to think at all, let alone
think about the crazy things that had happened, she found herself contemplating her role among the Horsemen. If she bore the
Scales and played the part of Famine, she was going to bring
chaos and pain to the world. And if she balked, Death was going
to let War slaughter her. Of course, the Red Rider might do that
anyway, depending on which way the wind blew.

And she thought she'd wanted to kill herself *before*. Lisa let
out a short, bitter laugh. She was so screwed.

When she finally got home, all she wanted to do was go up
to her bedroom and bury herself under her covers. Maybe she
could pray once more that this was all some weird Lexapro-
inspired dream. Mentally, she was tired of dwelling on food
and Famine; she was completely wrung out emotionally. And
physically, she wasn't much better: she was already exhausted
just from the short walk from Tammy's house to her own, and
far too thirsty—and so damn cold. A hot cup of tea (no sugar,
no milk) would do wonders, she decided.

Standing on the front steps, she realized she didn't have her
keys—or her purse. Of course she didn't; she'd dashed out of
the house to escape James and Suzanne, and she hadn't thought

to grab her jacket, let alone her shoulder bag. She'd been lucky that she was already wearing boots; otherwise she might have fled with only her thick socks covering her feet.

Midnight whinnied.

Lisa looked over her shoulder at the black horse. "I need a break."

The steed blinked its white eyes, as if in disbelief.

"I'll be out soon," she said, wishing it were a lie but feeling in her soul that it was God's own truth.

Midnight snorted, then trotted around the side of the house—probably to the garden, Lisa thought. The horse seemed to enjoy grazing. Maybe instead of pralines, she should get her steed a huge tossed salad.

Sighing, Lisa rang the doorbell. If her dad hadn't returned, she could always knock on their neighbor's door. She preferred to stay away from old Mrs. Rizzo, who was blue haired and had a tendency to want to stuff her visitors as if she were plumping them up for her oven. But Lisa would chance it if it meant getting the spare key. If only she were rebellious enough to keep her window unlocked and primed for sneaking out and in.

But the door swung open, cutting short her momentary desire for a life of juvenile delinquency. Lisa's words of thanks and greeting died in her throat.

In the doorway, her mother frowned at her. "No jacket, Lisabeth? You want to catch your death of cold?"

||||||

Lisa felt her mother's gaze riddling her back. She did her best to ignore it as she fixed her tea.

"That sweater is too big on you," her mother commented.

Lisa bristled. This is what her mother did: she nitpicked. Nothing was ever good enough, let alone just right. She'd grown up with the constant backhanded compliment, "If you'd just lose ten pounds, you'd be so beautiful." Well, she'd lost the ten pounds (and then some), but now her mother's criticism tended toward Lisa's sallow skin or her limp hair or her clothing.

"I like the sweater," Lisa said, sounding defensive to her own ears.

"It makes you look like some castaway refugee."

Lisa decided not to call her mother on mixing metaphors. Instead, she focused on dunking her tea bag into the mug of hot water.

"And those jeans. Really, Lisabeth. I realize that fashion today might lean toward the baggy, but those jeans are all but falling off you."

Lisa closed her eyes and tried to think of a happy place.

"I'd appreciate it if you acknowledged me when I speak to you."

Lisa swallowed her anger and dunked her tea bag. "Sorry."

She fished out the bag and dumped it in the garbage, then took her cup and tried to leave the kitchen.

"Sit with me," her mother commanded.

Damn it. Resigning herself to another lecture that pretended to be affectionate conversation, Lisa sank into one of the kitchen chairs. She must have pulled a muscle while riding on Midnight, because the act of sitting made her wince.

Sandy Lewis, however, didn't sit right away. She stood there, in her immaculate kitchen that gleamed with technological innovation and managed to sparkle with homespun charm:

top-of-the-line appliances balanced with quaint pictures of apples in baskets going for five cents a pound; caches of cutting boards that folded into drawers; grass-green cushions meant to soften the harsh angles of expensive chairs more at home in magazine spreads than in an actual home. Lisa's mom was as much a prop as the stove she rarely used: hair sculpted into perfect form and glued into place; fully made-up face from foundation to lip liner; a smart skirt-suit adorned with tasteful buttons; the matching accessories that carried the eye from head to ear to throat to wrists to fingers to legs; the shoes polished bright enough to blind. Perfectly groomed, perfectly poised, she had a calculating gaze and a smile as rare as spring snow.

Lisa sipped her tea. She'd seen it all before. She just hadn't planned on seeing it right now.

"Well." Mrs. Lewis took a seat opposite her daughter. "I'll be on the road in a few hours, so we have some time to talk."

Terrific. Lisa tried to keep the annoyance off her face. "I thought you were home early."

"Change of schedule."

"Ah." As if that explained anything. Not that Lisa cared; she'd been all but invisible to her mother for years now.

"So," Mrs. Lewis said, "where were you coming from?"

She wanted to tell her mother it was none of her business, that she should stop pretending she gave a damn about Lisa. But she couldn't stomach saying any of that. Sullen, Lisa replied, "Am I in trouble?"

"Lisabeth, I just want to know where you were out and about." She sounded annoyed, as if Lisa's question had offended her. "Don't I deserve to know that much about you, at least?"

Of course. It was always what her mother deserved. Lisa sighed. "I was at Tammy's."

"Oh." Impossible for one word to hold any more scorn. "I wish you wouldn't spend so much time with that girl."

Lisa grimaced. Her mom had never liked Tammy, probably because once she'd heard Tammy go on and on about how amazing Lisa's dad was. What did it say about her mother, Lisa wondered as she took another sip of tea, that she was insecure over a seventeen-year-old girl thinking her husband was terrific?

"I don't think I'll be hanging out with her anymore," Lisa said, muttering into her cup.

Her words must have caught Mrs. Lewis off-guard: her mother blinked in surprise, mascaraed lashes fluttering against her face like caffeinated spiders. "Well. What happened?"

Hunched over her mug of tea, Lisa gazed up at her mom. "She's phony."

The words hung in the air, Lisa's accusation all too clear.

Mrs. Lewis cleared her throat. "How's James?"

Lisa's chest tightened. Her voice flat, she said, "We got into a fight."

"Well. That's no surprise. You seem to be fighting quite a bit lately." Her mother spoke with a clinical detachment, as if discussing the flight pattern of Canadian geese. Lately, the only times Lisa heard her mother get passionate was when she was rehearsing her speeches for her various charity events. The other times, Lisa assumed her mother practiced meaningful smiles in front of the mirror; she certainly didn't waste them on her child.

"Whatever." Lisa just didn't care—about anything.

"You kids," Mrs. Lewis said with a verbal eye roll. "You always think everything is so important. So much drama."

That sparked a feeling: annoyance. Of course her mother was dismissive; Lisa's life wasn't large-scale enough for her mother to actually care about. "It was a *fight*."

"A fight," her mother repeated, then clucked her tongue. "Honestly, even if it is a real fight, which it probably isn't, that doesn't make it a war to win, Lisabeth."

War.

"It's not about *winning*," Mrs. Lewis continued. "It's about *communication*. About pulling yourself out of your own world-view and into someone else's perception. There are other people here besides you, you know."

"You've got no backbone to you," War says to Lisa, the knight's face hidden within the confines of her helmet. "Look at you: you're just a child. Practically a mouse."

Mrs. Lewis sniffed. "My goodness, Lisabeth. You don't have to look so stricken. No matter how badly your feelings got hurt, I'm sure you and James will kiss and make up. You always do."

Her mother prattled on, but Lisa had stopped listening. She was too busy thinking about the Red Rider on her warhorse, armor immaculate, the huge sword shining darkly, and her voice booming, promising to cut Lisa down.

And Lisa believed it.

Shivering, she took another sip of tea. No doubt about it: War was über-scary, and most likely insane. Probably all the battle lust, Lisa decided. That got her thinking about War as Death's handmaiden . . . as well as other things to (and with) Death. And *that* made Lisa feel completely squicked out. Yuck.

It was another minute before she realized her mother wasn't speaking any longer. She glanced up from her tea to see Mrs.

Lewis staring at her, almost squinting, her lipsticked mouth pulled down into a pensive frown.

God, she hated it when people looked at her as if she had a booger hanging from her nose. She snapped, "What?"

"You don't look good."

The Thin voice trilled, *You'd look so much better if you just lost ten pounds.*

Lisa gnashed her teeth, thinking, *Shut up, shut up, shut up!*

You're weak. A mouse, the Thin voice lamented. *Vermin.*

Her eyes closed, she imagined a field of rats, undulating and thick, their whiskers like sticks of grain.

"Lisa."

That pulled Lisa out of her feverish thoughts. Her mother never called her *Lisa,* not since she was a little girl. Once Lisa had developed breasts, her name had forever been *Lisabeth* to Sandy Lewis.

"You look sick," her mother said softly, as if she were actually concerned.

Lisa opened her eyes and regarded her mother. Her brow had—oh, shock and horror—*wrinkled* as her brows arched up. For that one moment, Sandy Lewis looked every year of her age.

"Your face is gaunt," Mrs. Lewis said, taking in her daughter's appearance. "Your eyes are sunken. You . . . my God, Lisa. You look terrible."

Terrible, the Thin voice agreed. *Huge and ugly and so* fat. *You're hopeless.*

Her mother spoke again tentativly. "Are you dieting?"

Lisa shrugged. She hadn't thought of her relationship with food as anything as simple as a diet, not in a long, long time.

A diet, she could break.

A diet is temporary, the Thin voice said knowingly. *Being thin is forever.*

Exactly. Forever. Lisa wanted to sob.

There was another long moment as her mother measured her up. Then something hardened in Sandy Lewis's eyes, and her mouth set itself back into its prim and proper line. "Well. You need to stop it," her mother declared, sitting back as if that were the end of it. "Clearly, you're not getting the nutrition you need. You should know better."

Lisa's heart galloped in her chest; her blood pounded in her ears. "What are you saying?"

"You're too thin, Lisabeth."

Oh my God.

Black was white. Heaven was hell. Her mother couldn't seriously have said she was too thin.

Lying, the Thin voice insisted, *she's lying she's just jealous like Tammy like Suzanne like all of them jealous that you have control over your body and they don't they don't they can only dream of doing what you do—*

"So whatever crazy diet you're on," her mother scolded, "you just stop it."

Lisa wanted to scream. *Just stop it,* her mother said, as if it were that easy. Lisa's hands shook, and tea lapped over the rim of her mug.

Her mother sniffed. "Or is it pills? I know a lot of girls like to take pills to curb their appetites."

"No pills," Lisa gritted. Not including the stolen Lexapro.

You couldn't even kill yourself, the Thin voice said, mocking and cold. *You're pathetic.*

"Is it the tea?" Her mother motioned to Lisa's cup. Bracelets clacked on her wrist. "You've been drinking tons of tea. Is it one of those herbal remedy things? Those are all a crock, you know. They just dehydrate you, and then you'll gain it all back when you drink water—"

"It's not the tea!" Lisa hefted her cup and hurled it at the floor. The mug shattered, spraying liquid and porcelain on the linoleum, splashing Lisa's pants. She shrieked, "It's not the fucking tea!"

Shocked in equal parts by her daughter's profanity as by her violence, Sandy Lewis clasped a hand to her breast and stammered, "Lisa! What's wrong with you?"

Everything. The Thin voice sighed. *Everything's wrong. You're a failure. You're fat. You're nothing.*

Lisa fisted her hands in her hair and pressed them against her head, screaming, trying to drown out the Thin voice. *Stop it!* she cried out, but her mouth wouldn't work. *Just stop it!*

She didn't feel it when she tore out hunks of her hair.

"Lisa!" Mrs. Lewis reached over to put a well-manicured hand on her daughter's shoulder. "Please, you're hurting yourself!"

Hurting? Oh, she had no idea what it felt like to be hurting.

But Lisa would show her.

Shadows ate her eyes and feasted on her soul as Lisabeth Lewis gave way to Famine. The Black Rider clamped a hand on to the woman's wrist—a woman who thought she could touch Famine and not be touched in return.

And Famine slowly sucked out Sandy Lewis's life.

Muscles atrophied and body fat melted away, leaving her skin loose and ill fitting over her frame. Her skin broke out into patches of dryness, then became peppered with red rashes. Sickness bloomed inside of her in black flowers of scurvy, of anemia, of beriberi and pellagra. As her body ate itself, her heart and lungs slowly shrank. Her bones became more and more prominent until they were clearly visible under her suit of flesh. Her stomach bloated as fluids collected within, desperately trying to keep her body functioning. Hollowed out from hunger, her eyes sank into their sockets, and her face transformed into a skeletal mask.

She opened her mouth to cry out in agony, but she was too weak to make any sound stronger than a wheeze. Dying, she held on to Famine's shoulder and croaked out her daughter's name.

Through the black haze of Famine, Lisa blinked. She saw her mother's desiccated form, and she whispered, "Mommy?"

Her mother's yellowed eyes rolled up. Shaking with palsy, she collapsed back into her chair.

"Mommy! Oh God oh God oh God . . ."

Lisa, sickened and horrified by what she'd done, clutched her mother's bony hand. She had to make it right. She had to fix it. Had to . . .

Her mother's energy swam inside of her, sang within her. Filled her almost to the bursting point. She had to get it out, had to . . .

She had to give it back.

Biting her lip, Lisa closed her eyes and reached inside herself. Her imaginary fingers dug deep, scrabbling to find the life she'd stolen, desperate for purchase. She gagged; she coughed. But she wouldn't let go—not of her mother's hand, not of her own power.

Give it back!!!

With a body-shaking heave, her power spewed out. It splashed against her mother, coating her face and hair, dripping down her throat. It sank into her, and Sandy Lewis absorbed it like a sponge, her body filling out, her organs rebuilding, her muscles reclaiming their shape. Disease burned away; her skin firmed up and smoothed out. Her face softened. And her eyes brimmed with tears.

Lisa smiled weakly, then sank back into her seat, shivering. She was ice all over, from her face to her toes. She was so horrifically hungry that the thought of food nauseated her. But she'd done it. She'd finally forced herself to purge.

Tammy would be proud, she thought, and then she let out a laugh that sounded like a whimper.

"Lisa," her mother said—her normal, healthy, self-centered superficial mother who didn't give a damn about her and who was too busy speaking out for causes to bother speaking to her daughter—and took Lisa's hand gently, as if worried it would break. "There's something wrong with you."

Lisa was too exhausted to nod her agreement.

"You're sick," her mother said.

Yes, she was. But Lisa also was hopeful. Not for herself, no; she was a lost cause, and had been for far too long. But maybe she could help make things better.

"Bed," she whispered, trying to pull herself to her feet. Things went gray for a moment, and then her mother was right there, propping her up, letting Lisa lean heavily on her.

Under her brittle, perfect shell, her mother was surprisingly soft.

Sandy Lewis helped her daughter up the stairs, even stripped the boots off her feet. Lisa was already fast asleep when her mother tucked her into bed, and so she didn't feel the gentle kiss on her forehead, nor the careful smudging of a finger over her brow, trying to remove the lipstick print.

CHAPTER 14

Lisa walks amidst green and yellow fields, the stalks standing a little taller as she passes by. Ahead of her, she sees waves of darkness attempting to drown the crops—rats feasting, disease spreading.

She smiles. She won't allow such things to hurt the food. She will keep the food safe and give the food to the world.

Raising her arm, she summons the Scales. They appear, heavy in her hand, and she grips them tightly, taking comfort from their weight. Weight gives substance; weight allows you to plant your feet and meet the broaching storm. Light spills forth from the Scales, illuminating her path as, smiling, she walks on, unperturbed.

Thousands of red eyes peer at her; thousands of mouths flash wickedly sharp teeth. Their bodies are infested with viruses and bacteria, promising sickness and death with just one bite.

Lisa's smile broadens.

As one, the rats charge forward, swarming her.

Lisa holds the Scales high. The light is blinding, and burning, and with it comes a surge of pure delight. The smell of charred flesh tickles her nostrils; squeals of dying vermin make the sweetest music.

As one, the rats perish.

Around her, the fields reach up to the heavens and try to touch the sun.

It was a good dream, and it ended much too soon, as good dreams are wont to do.

When Lisa opened her eyes, it was the middle of the night. She groaned, hurting all over, thinking she needed to take a hot shower and work out the kinks—and knowing in her heart that a shower wouldn't help. She was sick, feverish. She wanted water, but the thought of getting up made her sigh. She was too tired to move. Exhausted, Lisa closed her eyes and wondered how she would manage to get out of bed.

Time passed.

She must have fallen asleep again, because when she next opened her eyes, the covers had been kicked off. Lisa glanced down, surprised to find that she was still dressed. Her thoughts were soupy and slow, but she thought she remembered her mother helping her up the stairs.

Wow. She must *really* be sick. Either she had been hallucinating, or her mother had actually been worried about her.

Her lips twitched into a brief smile, which then turned into a grimace. Her lips were cracked and dry, and her mouth was so parched that when she swallowed, it burned her throat. Her heart couldn't seem to find the right rhythm in her chest; it stuttered and skipped around, fiddling to find the right music. And, Lisa realized with dismay, it actually hurt to breathe, as if her lungs couldn't inflate properly.

Well, she thought, her hand shaking as she mopped her sweating brow. *This isn't good.*

Vaguely, she remembered having tea, and then listening to her mom lecture her about how terrible her clothing was, and . . .

Her eyes widened. And she'd hurt her mother. She'd used Famine against her and made her starve.

But she's okay, she told herself firmly. *She's okay. I remember, I helped her. I made her healthy again—*

Oh.

Oh!

A grin spread across her face, and it didn't matter that it hurt her cheeks. She'd helped! She could use Famine to actually help people . . . just like the White Rider had insinuated! She wasn't a monster. She . . .

Her stomach whined, a low-pitched plaintive cry for food.

Yes, she needed to eat. Not for herself, no—God, she didn't think she'd ever be able to eat for herself again—but for others. She had to fuel herself. She had to store up enough energy so she could give it back.

She had to get up.

It took Lisa five minutes to gather enough strength to roll over. Then she needed to catch her breath. It occurred to her that she might be dying.

Well, she thought, *if Death shows up, I'll just tell him he needs to wait.*

Slowly, she made her way out of bed, and she nearly collapsed when she stood up. She was dizzy, and so very tired. But she had to get downstairs and fix herself something to eat.

No, the Thin voice lamented, *you can't eat. You need to be thin.*

Shut up, she told the Thin voice. What she needed was energy. And that meant she had to eat. Somehow.

It took her a small eternity to navigate her way down the stairs.

In the kitchen, she didn't bother with the light. Her thick socks padding her footsteps, Lisa went to the refrigerator and forced it open. The thought of actually eating anything was enough to make her stomach pitch and roll.

But she could drink.

She grabbed one of her mother's protein drinks, a berry and yogurt concoction that promised to taste like "real strawberries," according to the label. Good; she wouldn't want to drink anything that tasted like fake strawberries. By the light of the open refrigerator, she opened the bottle and brought it to her lips.

And she nearly gagged from the smell.

Okay, she thought, *I can do this.*

Taking a deep breath through her mouth, she tilted the bottle back and forced the drink down her throat. The yogurt coated her tongue and was so thick as it slid down that she thought she was choking. She swallowed, and swallowed again—and again, commanding herself to keep it down, to somehow keep it all down.

When the bottle was empty, she dropped it to the ground. Her breath stank of fermented milk and spoiled berries. She pushed against the refrigerator door so that it closed, then teetered her way to the back door in the kitchen.

Her scalp hurt from where she'd pulled out fistfuls of hair. Her throat burned. Tears stung her eyes. Her heart threatened to stutter to a halt.

And yet, as Lisabeth Lewis opened the door and saw the black horse gaze upon her, she was grinning. Not caring that she wasn't wearing shoes or a jacket, she slowly approached her steed.

"Hey there," she said. "Miss me?"

The steed nickered. It seemed to return her grin as it lowered itself to the ground.

Lisa fumbled her way atop Midnight's back. Once seated, she threaded her fingers through the blue-black mane. "Let's go," she said.

Midnight whinnied its approval, and the two took off into the night.

|||||

From above, the pyramids looked like children's toys someone had accidentally dropped in the desert. The Sphinx was an afterthought.

Midnight swooped down, and soon they flew over a bustling city of browns and reds, a huge tower piercing the haze and smog, a concrete needle among the paper diamonds of wind-kissed kites. Pigeons played tag, darting out and soaring between bits of twine and plastic, avoiding satellite dishes and eventually finding their way back to their keepers' boxes. Below, houses were a mishmash of wood and brick, with various silver domes and mud brown mosques here and there. Shopping centers, both cosmopolitan and traditional, ran parallel throughout the city, the name-brand stores sitting side by side with fruit vendors.

The city teemed with life. People dotted the rooftops, flying kites and catching the breeze. Teenagers filled the alleys, gossiping and kissing. Adults walked in the streets, ambling along with goats and roosters, motorcycles weaving between them, taxis vying for parking spots with donkeys.

Lisa was enthralled. She saw groups of boys laughing as they passed bowls between them, heard women's buzzing chatter as they talked on their cell phones while hanging laundry. Girls lapped up ice cream; men held cigarettes in one hand and cups of tea in the other. A mixture of smells hit her: cumin and falafel, the press of human bodies, exhaust and animal dung, all weaving together into an exotic perfume. Lisa breathed in the city air and held it deep within her, feeling it fill her like magic.

The horse touched down, and they walked along the maze of streets. She saw walls lined with gold trinkets and brass plates; she was dazzled by gemstones in jewelry shop windows. Bolts of material cascaded around her, sequined and smooth. Statues of small gods stood guard against tourists and hawkers and city folk. Hundreds of shops called out for attention, offering linens and lamps, shoes and candleholders, tables, chairs, rugs and clothing and pipes and food . . . everything. Lisa grinned, euphoric.

Farther they walked, invisible, and now Lisa saw the reality rubbing through the storybook façade: the ramshackle roofs and patchwork walls, the piles of cinder block and stone in the street covered with dust, the shop owners waiting outside their stores to entice passersby to step inside, the lines of clothing on display on hooks from above packed together tightly, throngs of people milling about the street like something out of a pickpocket's fantasy. More than the excitement, Lisa now felt pangs of boredom, of desperation, of hopeless dreams.

Outside a fruit and vegetable market, Lisa spied a boy, painfully thin, eyeing the mangoes hanging in bags and the rows of dates and figs on display. His gaze lingered on buckets of strawberries and plump oranges, on cartons of lettuce and bags of colorful peppers. She felt his gnawing hunger and understood he hadn't eaten a full meal in three days.

"Here," she said to Midnight. "Stop here, please."

The horse halted and knelt down in the dusty road. Lisa slid off and tested her legs; it wouldn't do for her to kick off her good deed by tripping over her own feet and getting a mouthful of dirt for her trouble. *Balance,* she told herself. Taking a breath, Lisa approached the boy.

Like the hordes of people around her, he didn't notice her or the black steed. Even if she hadn't had some sort of invisibility system going on, he probably wouldn't have seen her—he was far too focused on the tantalizing fruits and vegetables, and on the shopkeeper who was eyeballing him. The boy slouched, hands shoved deep into his pockets, his mouth fixed in a resigned frown. His body language screamed "shoplifter," but his eyes looked haunted and sad.

Lisa felt bad for him. He couldn't have been more than ten. He should have been playing video games and reading comic books, not contemplating how to pinch a mango.

Pausing for a moment, Lisa focused on the baskets of strawberries, thinking about the taste of the yogurt drink she'd choked down. She closed her eyes and reached inward, searching for the part of her that was Famine. Sweat beaded on her brow as she concentrated, swaying where she stood. She gasped as she touched the black power within her, pulsing and hungry. Her fists clenching, she imagined pouring that energy into the grim-faced boy.

It fought her at first, snarling and snapping. Lisa stood her ground, and with a roar, the power surged out of her in a black wave, dousing the boy.

He spluttered and shook, gasping. And then a delighted grin broke across his face. The gut-wrenching hunger was gone! He could think clearly again, praise Allah! The boy ran off, feeling better than he had in months, ever since his stonecutter father lost his job and daily meals became a thing of fond memory.

Lisa sagged against her steed, exhausted. The horse chided her as it nuzzled against her palm, scolding her with its white-eyed gaze for wasting her energy—or maybe for using Famine in such a productive way. She didn't know; unlike Death, she didn't speak Horse.

She absently rubbed Midnight's side, taking comfort from its warmth. Even though she was utterly wrecked, she was positively giddy. She'd helped the boy. He wouldn't need to eat for at least a day, maybe even two. She knew this just as she knew two plus two equaled four. The effort hadn't been as harmful to her as it had been when she'd helped her mother; then again, she hadn't first tried to kill the boy.

She flushed from guilt. Some people only *thought* they had a killer temper.

As if sensing her distress, Midnight whinnied softly.

"I'm okay," she said, lying only a little. She'd work off her guilt, like a penance. She could help more people. Yes—that was exactly what she would do. But first, she needed to eat.

No, the Thin voice whispered, *don't do that.*

Lisa stiffened. *You don't get a vote,* she thought angrily at the Thin voice. She tried not to worry that she was talking to herself. In the past few days, she'd gotten a flying horse and the power to suck out people's health; what was a little thing like possible schizophrenia?

You're weak, the Thin voice whispered.

Yes, she was . . . but in a different way than the Thin voice insinuated. Lisa was having a hard time standing.

Midnight nickered again, then turned around to face Lisa. The steed gently placed its mouth around her wrist, careful not to bite her. Then it knelt down. Lisa had no choice but to follow the horse. She sat on the dusty road. Around her, people walked on, oblivious.

Once she was seated, the horse removed its mouth. It snorted, as if to tell her to stay there. Then her steed walked over to the fruit and vegetable stand, its hooves coughing up dust. It leaned over the orange bin, rummaging. All the while, the stall-keeper hawked his wares to passersby.

When her steed approached Lisa, it had a huge orange between its teeth. It dropped the fruit into her lap, then went back to the market. Lisa used her sweater to wipe horse saliva from the orange (*ew, gross*), then peeled off the rind with shaking fingers. She broke off a section of the fruit and popped it into her mouth.

Her taste buds stood up and cheered, then did a happy dance.

She chewed, savoring the citrus tang, the burst of sweetness on her tongue. She swallowed and thought she'd gone to heaven. God, it was so . . . damn . . . good! Greedy, she ate the rest of the orange so quickly that juice dribbled down her chin. When she finished, Midnight had a basket of strawberries waiting for her.

And so it went: the horse fetched her food and she ate it. When she no longer thought she might faint, she shared the fruit with her steed. It munched on figs and dates while she gobbled peppers and more oranges, vaguely recalling saying something to her father about preferring to eat five oranges than to drink one glass of orange juice.

Soon she felt strong enough to stand, and soon after that, to ride. As Lisa and Midnight picked their way along the labyrinth-like streets, she knew where she needed to go next. She was full of food, and she was ready to give it back to those who needed it. Dimly, she wondered how long she would be able to do the Good Samaritan thing before her body gave out. If she saw a man with long blond hair sitting on a pale horse, she'd turn the other way.

Before anything else, she had a promise to keep.

"I want to go to a place that's already been visited by Famine," she told her steed. "A place where the people are really hurting. Starving. Can you do that?"

The black horse snorted its answer: of course it could.

"All right, that's great," she said, scratching Midnight behind its ears. "Before we go, there's something we still have to do while we're here."

The horse sniffed its question.

"You'll see," she replied.

They walked along the marketplace until Lisa found what she'd been looking for: a patisserie. There in the window she saw cakes and pastries and chocolates—including boxes of pralines, with the individual chocolates shaped like Ramses II and Cleopatra.

Midnight's ears quivered.

"I'll be right back," she said, sliding off the horse with no help at all. "I have to pick up some chocolate."

Lisa didn't know that horses could salivate.

She slipped into the shop and grabbed two boxes of pralines. Neither the seller nor the customers saw her. Lisa felt a stab of guilt as she exited the store, but two things helped her cope: first, she was Famine, damn it, and so she was doing her job by taking food; second, the look on Midnight's face was worth it.

Outside the patisserie, Lisa sat on the dusty ground and watched, smiling, as her horse set to the chocolates, letting out equine sounds of contentment as it ate.

CHAPTER 15

They traveled. Galloping among the clouds, it occurred to Lisa that she was becoming rather blasé about riding horseback in the air.

It also occurred to her that she had, somewhere along the way, completely lost her mind.

She closed her eyes, trusting her steed to take her where she needed to go. Until they arrived, she would enjoy the feeling of the wind in her hair, of the horse's powerful body working hard beneath her. Fingers entwined tightly in Midnight's mane, her knees pressed against Midnight's ribs, Lisa held on.

And she grinned because, you know, it really was freaking cool.

|||||

It was another town that Lisa didn't recognize, a place with homes made of concrete walls and tin roofs, of cardboard shacks outfitted with plastic sheets. The ground was a paste of mud and rock. Drainage ditches overflowed, clogged with raw sewage. Dozens of small fires choked the air with the greasy black smoke from tires and other refuse burning lazily. A bony dog lapped at the tainted water that had pooled in the road, where some adults stood bathing listlessly. Children avoided the pigs rooting about trash piles. Flies hovered. Odors mingled, weaving together in a heated haze and floating upward, assaulting Lisa's nose.

Midnight touched down, its gallop slowing to a cantor and then to a walk. Lisa gazed upon the townsfolk, the scattered clusters of people shuffling about, zombielike, some wearing brightly colored shirts that belied the washed-out look in their eyes. A group of women wearing head scarves waited outside a building—some standing, others leaning against the decrepit walls, still others sitting, their faces half hidden by their hands as they prayed or napped or wept. Men sat outside empty shops, scowling, casting glares at the passersby and at the police driving by on patrol.

Yes, Famine had been here before. Its scars were everywhere, spread like pockmarks on the face of the town.

Heading toward the outskirts, past the loose rocks and flooded crops and muddy rivers, rows of women marched with straw baskets and oversize bundles balanced on their heads, trekking to work or, perhaps, to market. Lisa's mind flashed on the Disney movie *Snow White and the Seven Dwarfs*, when the dwarfs sang "Heigh-Ho!" as they exited the diamond mines. Disgusted with herself, Lisa looked away.

And she locked gazes with a skeletal child dressed in rags.

His—her? Lisa couldn't tell—eyes were bulbous, huge, filled with pain and resignation that no one, let alone a child, should ever have to encounter. Clutching a cookie, the child stared up at Lisa.

"You can see me?" she asked, stunned.

The child didn't reply, but the huge eyes blinked.

Lisa slid off her steed and approached the child slowly, her hand out, palm up, as if encountering a dog. "It's okay," she murmured. "I promise, I won't hurt you."

The child sighed, and Lisa's heart broke.

For the second time that night, she reached within herself and touched the power of Famine, then grabbed hold and pulled. It wrestled with her, trying to slip away, but Lisa held fast. Either Famine was growing used to her, or she was getting better at controlling it, for this time it didn't snap at her like a rabid hound. That didn't mean it was easy, not by any stretch; Lisa trembled from exertion and sweat beaded on her brow.

I can do this.

Her teeth clenched, she extended her power outward, shaping it into a funnel and touching it to the child's mouth in a gesture as gentle as a mother's kiss.

The child closed its eyes, perhaps waiting for the inevitable.

Slowly, Lisa released the energy within her, trickling it into the starving child. *Careful,* she told herself, *careful . . . Can't go too fast.* Gnashing her teeth until her molars screamed, Lisa bled life into the child, drop by drop. And then she hit the saturation point.

The girl—yes, a girl; Lisa knew that now—snapped her eyes open with a gasp, finding for the first time in her short life, her belly didn't ache. She placed a tiny hand on her swollen stomach, wondering at the sense of fullness.

Yes. Oh thank you, yes.

Sweating and shaking, Lisa cut off the power flow and let the funnel dissipate. The line connecting her to the girl snapped, and Lisa staggered backward, nearly stumbling into the muck of the street. Finding her balance, she pressed a hand against her forehead until she no longer felt dizzy.

Being a Good Samaritan, she decided, was harder than it looked.

She kept her head down until the world caught up to her. When she finally lowered her hand and looked up, she found the child standing in front of her, smiling.

Offering Lisa her cookie.

Lisa's breath caught in her throat, and her heart swelled like an orchestra's crescendo. Okay, maybe being a Good Samaritan was hard, but *wow*—in this moment, it was worth it.

Swallowing back tears, Lisa smiled and accepted the gift, suddenly famished. She bit down and chewed, then nearly spat it out—Famine identified the ingredients as a mixture of vegetable fat, salt, and dirt.

Dirt cookies, she thought numbly, staring at the food in her hand. *This girl has been eating dirt cookies.*

The child watched, her large eyes expectant.

Still smiling, Lisa forced the "treat" down; she even mimed rubbing her belly and made a yummy sound. The child grinned, revealing two baby teeth. With a look of extreme satisfaction, she toddled off, her rags slipping off her bony shoulders. Lisa watched until the child disappeared from view.

Midnight snorted.

"You can criticize, if you'd like," Lisa murmured. "I'm glad we helped."

The horse snorted again.

Lisa turned to face those white, skeptical eyes. "Hey, you had pralines."

Her steed fixed her with its milky gaze, then flicked its ears, abashed.

"I'm glad you liked them." Lisa patted the horse's powerful neck, wondering what to do next. She wouldn't have enough energy to help even a handful of people here, let alone everyone.

But she could try. The youngest children, at least, she could help—some of them, anyway.

After one last pat of Midnight's neck, she began to pick her way around the muddy patches of the road, intending to approach the myriad of mostly naked children swarming around garbage heaps. It was nasty, and rancid—the stench made her eyes water—but she could always shower when she got home.

Lisa halted in her tracks. A man off to the side of the road had caught her eye. He was dumping what looked like grass shavings onto the ground, adding to an already large pile.

Curious, she walked closer. The pile wasn't grass, she realized, but string beans, or something similar . . .

She squinted, taking in the long, wet stalks, and then she knew. The part of her that was Famine identified it as rice plants—specifically, rice from a submerged paddy.

Famine showed her how the seeds had been planted in small beds and then put into plowed, waterlogged fields. Later, the rice would have been harvested. In her mind, Lisa could see the farmers with their knives, tying the rice stalks into bundles and leaving them in their fields so that they'd dry before they were threshed, and then the new grain would again be dried.

But the problem here had been all the rain; twenty days of freak rains, drowning plants, washing away the livestock, caving in homes. Famine showed her the destructive sheets of rain, the rising ground water, the desperate townsfolk in their leaking shacks. Rice, unlike other crops, thrived in standing water. But if the rice was kept completely submerged for more than a few days, the plants would die.

Lisa knew this. Famine had told her. Famine understood food intimately, and on a deep level, so did Lisa.

Brown rice, the Thin voice whispered. *One hundred thirty-five calories.*

Shut up. Lisa watched the farmer laying out the dying rice plants, feverishly working to dry them in the hopes of saving some of his harvest so that he and his family wouldn't starve. He had to dry the plants. His desperation glowed around him in a black nimbus.

Lisa smiled. She was thirsty, anyway; that dirt cookie had been horribly dry and salty.

Heedless of her shoeless feet, she walked through the mud to get to the small area of road where the farmer toiled. The sun had baked this small patch of ground to hard clay. Spread out on the road, the rice plants looked faded and overboiled, like some of her mother's attempts at string beans.

Lisa crouched down, ignoring the farmer who was adding to the pile of drowned plants. Frowning with concentration, she touched one of the limp rice stems. She felt the excess moisture, heard the plant crying out for the sun. She imagined sucking that wetness from the rice, from all the rice, pulling it into her, quenching her thirst. And Famine drank.

The rice slowly dried.

At one point, Midnight had walked over to her, positioning itself to shield Lisa from the blasting sun. She barely noticed. Famine drank, and Lisa shivered from the cold.

Soon other men joined the farmer, adding their own wet bundles to the heap. They chatted, animated and pointing, and the first farmer removed his dry stash to let the others have more room.

Lisa's head jerked up, and she blinked furiously. Why had she been nodding off? Where was she? Panicking, she darted her gaze about, not understanding why there were painfully thin men and women near her, carting away bundles of grass out of the road. Her vision blurred, and when she stood tall, her stomach and legs rebelled, stabbing her. She doubled over, nauseated and cramping. *What's happening?* she wanted to shout, but her teeth were chattering and she was panting and nothing made any sense . . .

She nearly screamed when a horse neighed right behind her.

Scrabbling up, she cocked her fist back and then froze, staring at the large black horse with glowing white eyes. It cocked its head, as if asking a question.

"I know you," she said slowly. "I . . ."

She was drowning. She had to get the water out. She . . .

She was going to vomit.

She staggered toward the refuse pile, lightheaded and too far gone to be bothered by the flies or the stench. The children there didn't see her, except for one wide-eyed little girl who would grow up to be a powerful Mambo and keep the balance between the spirits and her people.

Lisa crashed to her knees.

The force inside of her surged up and fountained out in a massive spray of power and energy. Life—it washed over the children and the hogs and the garbage, plumping up both humans and animals and transforming fetid refuse into fertilizer ready to be given back to the land.

Exhausted and weak, Lisa slumped to the ground. Around her, children laughed for the first time in months as they danced on newly strong legs. Parents cried from joy as they hugged their babies, suddenly healthy, and gave their thanks to the powerful *loa* who'd blessed their children. Farmers sang as they collected their saved harvest.

They wouldn't starve. Not today, anyway.

Midnight bumped its nose against Lisa's back.

"I'm okay," she croaked. "Just tired."

The steed nickered softly, its breath tickling her ear.

"Yeah. Okay. I'm getting up."

She slowly pulled herself to her knees, and once again she found the little girl looking up at her, a radiant smile on her small face. The girl pointed at Lisa, then looked over her shoulder.

Behind her, a crowd of people held armfuls of red and white flowers.

Lisa said, "What . . . ?"

As if waiting for her acknowledgment, the little girl nodded.

The people approached, hesitantly, reverently, and as they bowed their heads low, they gently placed the flowers at the base of the fertilizer pile. On they came, men and women, old and young, their bodies hardened from a difficult life of toil and uncertainty, raining flowers from their fingers. Soon there was a pile of blossoms that reached Lisa's shins.

Her vision blurry with tears, Lisa said, "For me?"

The little girl smiled.

Overcome, Lisa cried, her tears running into her mouth as she laughed. They were thanking her. She'd helped them, and they were thanking her. Her chest burned with pride.

Her hands trembling, she reached out to touch the flowers. And Famine ate.

When the flowers all disappeared, the people cheered. They returned to their homes, searching for candles and rum, clothing themselves in white, ready to give thanks to the powerful spirits that had saved their children and their rice.

Lisa, alone except for Midnight, let out a burp. She tasted flowers on her tongue.

"Excuse me," she said, pulling herself to her feet. Then she giggled, utterly giddy. That had been all sorts of awesome. Well, not the burp, but everything else. She'd helped those people, and they'd thanked her. Grinning madly, she reached out to stroke Midnight's neck. She could help other towns; she could slowly make her way across the world and ease its hunger . . .

The black horse stiffened, then bared its teeth.

"Midnight? What's wrong?"

A shadow fell over her, bringing with it the smell of old blood and new steel.

"Mouse," a woman's voice hissed, "just what do you think you're doing?"

Chapter 16

Oh God.

Terror gripped Lisa, squeezing her lungs and stealing her breath. She tried to swallow, but her throat was too thick with fear.

War had come for her.

She felt the Red Rider's presence radiating behind her, unadulterated rage hitting her back like the blast of an oven's heat. It was the snarl of a berserker, the breath of a tornado, the deadly promise of a monster in the closet, waiting for her to close her eyes. It was primal and furious, and it threatened to stop Lisa's heart.

Midnight stepped forward and let out a neigh of challenge. Another horse answered, its voice a bone-deep rumble. It was a sound filled with scorn and violence, and it turned Lisa's legs to gelatin.

I'm going to die.

She wanted to swoon, to close her eyes and pray to wake up, to scream for her mother to help her, to beg for James to arrive like a white knight and save her. She wanted to run, to hide, to melt away from the world. She wanted to be invisible and unimportant again. She wanted it all to go away.

She screwed her eyes closed and hoped that dying wouldn't hurt too much. Death seemed like a nice guy; maybe dying would be soft like a kiss. Maybe he'd sing to her before sending her on to eternal sleep.

"Well," Death says, "if you want to get all melodramatic about it. Do you want to die?"

Did she want to die?

In the darkness of her mind, she saw the little girl's wide-eyed face, her joyous smile. She tasted a cookie made of dirt and vegetable fat and salt. She smelled flowers given in thanks. She heard the sounds of a village no longer crying from hunger and fear, heard instead the footsteps of people lost in a celebratory dance, heard the rhythm of drums and flesh.

Lisa straightened her spine.

"We destroy," Pestilence says. "That's all we've ever done."

And she had, hadn't she? She'd destroyed the water that had blighted the crops. She'd destroyed the hunger that had been eating those children alive. She'd destroyed, and the people here would live.

She'd done that. She, Lisabeth Lewis, seventeen and anorexic and suicidal and uncertain of her own path—she'd done something that mattered. She'd ignored her own pain and had helped others.

Maybe she wanted to live after all.

Death's voice came, still and small, and so close it was as if he were right beside her: *Chin up, Black Rider.*

Lisa lifted her chin, then turned around to face the fiery gaze of War.

‖‖‖

The mouse looked as if she'd keel over and die.

War snorted, a sound echoed by the red steed standing to her left. How could Death have gifted such a weak-kneed girl with the phenomenal power of a Horseman? War shook her head. No matter how long she rode, she would never understand the Pale Rider.

Of course, most creatures didn't understand Death.

The two steeds faced off, posturing and challenging, as War waited for the girl to turn around (for even one such as she wouldn't stab an unarmed opponent in the back). She loomed over the girl. She didn't even need her Sword to kill her; she could lift the mouse by the hair and thigh and snap her spine over a bent knee. Or maybe she'd just twist the girl's neck until that sweet snap filled War's ears.

Yes. She'd do it quick. The girl was a Horseman, however unbelievable that was. Out of courtesy for the office, War would make it quick. She smiled, moved by her own magnanimity. All good wars had rules, after all. Even the Red Rider followed a certain decorum.

Something happened, then, as War flexed her hands and imagined the feeling of the girl's neck between her powerful fingers: the frail thing that was currently Famine paused in her quaking and sweating.

War arched a brow. Curious. Perhaps the girl was praying; her fear-stench had slowly given way to the subtle aroma of reflection. A smile flitted across War's mouth, hidden by her helmet. She had little patience for religion (although she approved heartily of the religious fanatics who sought to cleanse the world of heresy), and the only faith War had was in cold steel and hot blood.

Three heartbeats later, the mouse stood taller. And damned if now she didn't reek of the spicy scent of determination.

Most interesting. War waited to see what the girl would do.

The mouse turned around, her head held high, her hands fisted by her sides. She no longer looked like a victim, War noticed. She had an aura of confidence that hadn't been there before, a quiet acceptance of inner strength and peace.

War had no patience at all for peace.

"I'm helping people," the girl said in a voice that didn't waver, a voice that sounded nothing like that of the scared little thing War had found outside a restaurant in Sydney, sick from her own power.

"Are you?" War replied, bemused despite herself. She was still going to kill the impudent thing—she wasn't about to deal with another Famine who didn't know her place—but first she could amuse herself with talk; a game, appropriately enough, of cat and mouse.

Stroking the naked Sword that was her symbol of office, War regarded the newest Famine. Yes, the girl had found her backbone. War supposed she could respect that, however grudgingly. She found no sport in slaughtering the weak.

The mouse stared back brazenly, her power's black touch already leaking into her eyes. They glittered, birdlike, as she looked back at War. The Red Rider paused. For a moment, it seemed the girl was contemplating how War would taste.

Within her helm, War grinned. So the mouse thought she was a tiger, eh?

"I am," the girl said, as if in answer to War's thought. "And I'm afraid there won't be any fighting on the menu today."

The grin faded. "Is that so, Mouse?"

"It is."

No longer amused, War decided to end the game. "You think you know the fate of this flyspeck village? Another day or month of food, and you think you've saved them all?" War snorted her derision. "You're even more of an idiot than I'd thought."

The mouse flared her nostrils, but she didn't reply.

"I've been working here for decades," War growled, her voice dripping scorn like blood from a pierced heart, "slowly enticing the people here to give in to their primal natures."

"People have all sorts of natures," the girl said. "All sorts of appetites."

War chuckled, low and lush. "Yes, appetites. You weren't here for the food riots, Mouse. They were glorious. Shops looted. Cars burned. People died, ripped apart in the fray. The peacekeepers gassed the protesters, shot them with rubber bullets that left them battered and broken." War smiled at the memory. "People get violent when they're hungry."

"Sometimes," the mouse said, "they just get stupid."

War's mouth dropped open. "You *dare?*"

"You should leave now," the girl said, her voice dreamlike. "You're not welcome here."

War was too furious to be shocked. She bellowed, "You think you can reverse all I've done here? You think you can banish War from this place? Think again, girl!" With a snarl, War brandished the Sword, holding it high. "You can't banish *me*. The *world* is my domain. I own everything I look at!"

The girl had the audacity to smile. "Do you now?"

War's vision clouded in a red mist. She was going to kill the girl slowly. She was going to carve her like a turkey and feed chunks of her body to the red warhorse.

"I do," War growled. "I always have. War is every human's birthright. Man against man, man against woman, man against animal, man against nature—it's all war." She grinned, her teeth sharp, her lip pulped and bloody. "I am *everywhere,* girl. Who are you, to think you could ever threaten *me?*"

The mouse—no, not a mouse at all, War noted through the red fury of her vision, but the Horseman of Famine—spread her hands, and shadows crawled up her arms as if in answer to her summons, flowing over her shoulders and down her torso and legs and feet, clothing her in a coat and pants and boots of darkness. Beneath a wide-rimmed black hat, her obsidian eyes crackled with power. And in her black-gloved hand, the Scales shone brightly.

"I am Famine," the Black Rider said. "And I'm telling you to get your armored ass out of here before I suck you dry."

"Oh," War said with a laugh, smiling as she lost herself to the blood lust that would give her the power to kill and kill and kill. "You just made the last mistake of your feeble little life."

With a roar, War charged.

⦀⦀

It was like something out of a dream. Lisa had decided she wanted to live, and she'd turned to face War. And as she'd stared up at the warrior woman—the one who'd promised her death, the one who criticized and controlled and sought to dominate through fear—she realized she was gazing upon the embodiment of the Thin voice.

Pestilence had told her so: *"War has been known to twist things her own way."* Yes, that was the Thin voice.

Death had told her so, and more plainly: *"She can be brutal. She likes to draw it out. Slowly. And rather painfully."* And that was the Thin voice, too.

And War herself, of course. From atop her red steed, War had decreed it: *Mind your betters.* Oh, that was the Thin voice, telling her again and again that Lisa was nothing, was worthless, was pathetic.

Lisa was sick of the Thin voice. She was sick of being bullied, of being told she wasn't good enough, of feeling horrible about herself and about her life, of being helpless.

Of being a mouse.

And with that, Lisa was no longer afraid of War, or of the Thin voice, or of life. Lisa spoke to War, telling her that she, Lisabeth Lewis, was helping people and that there wouldn't be any fighting on the menu today. (She'd thought that particularly clever, what with her being Famine.)

War hadn't thought Lisa especially clever. War had shouted, and blustered, and threatened. Blah, blah, blah. Lisa tried talking to her, but really, it was rather funny watching this looming presence be reduced to nothing more than Shakespearean sound and fury.

So Lisa had smiled.

And then War raised her sword high—her *Sword,* Lisa understood, War's symbol of office—and Lisa knew that War intended to cut her down where she stood.

"You are full of fear," Death says, *"when instead you should be comfortable with your own strength."*

And she was, Lisa realized, her smile broadening. For the first time since the Thin voice had whispered to her, Lisabeth Lewis welcomed her own inner strength.

With that acceptance, she welcomed the power that flooded her. Black on black on black, Famine rippled over her, transforming her into a Horseman. In her hand, the Scales gleamed.

Once again, the voices of the world opened up to her, but they were no longer screaming. They were humming, singing, filling her with energy. They were the voices of the hungry, beckoning to her like friends, compelling her to feed them.

Grinning madly at the Red Rider, Famine declared her challenge.

And War charged.

⦚⦚⦚⦚⦚

Later, the people would tell the tale of the Shadow and the Fire, the story of the two *loa* who fought for the souls of those living in the war-torn, hungry land.

The Mambo would recount the battle, and listeners would grip their white candles, heedless of the hot wax spilling onto their fingers, their bodies swaying to the rhythm of the Mambo's words and the drums thumping like a heartbeat.

The people would listen, enthralled. For when *loa* battle, the world stands still and all living things tremble as they wait for judgment.

⦚⦚⦚⦚⦚

War surged forward, the Sword high and already arcing to cut Lisa in two. Lisa threw herself to the side just before the weapon sliced down. She hit the muddy ground and rolled, clutching the Scales to her chest until she was back on her feet, her symbol of office held in front of her, glowing with power.

Lisa had time to notice three things.

One: She wasn't dead. Actually, she'd just moved like some

sort of ninja superhero. How freaking awesome was that? If she weren't so busy trying to stay alive, she would have cheered.

Two: She was wearing a killer black outfit, complete with hat, gloves, and boots. Who knew that Famine could make such a fashion statement?

Three: The two steeds were fighting, all hooves and teeth, and if Lisa didn't want to get trampled to death she had better stay on the far left of what had turned into a battlefield.

Speaking of staying alive . . . yikes. As Lisa had been fascinated over the various perks that came with being Famine, War regained her balance. She drew the large sword back two handedly, like a baseball bat, and whirled to knock Lisa out of the ballpark—in pieces.

Lisa dropped down, crouching and planting her left hand on the ground for balance, thinking, *Crap crap crap crap.* This part wasn't so cool. Actually, this part was scary.

Be comfortable with your own strength.

Lisa didn't know whether that was just her memory of Death or whether the man himself was speaking in her mind. It didn't matter. Clenching her teeth to keep from screaming, Lisa surrendered herself to her power, allowed herself to trust Famine. It welcomed her with a black embrace, sliding into her mind like a hot knife through butter.

The Scales, Famine told her.

Scales. Got it. Lisa held the symbol aloft like a shield as War brought her own weapon down in a killing stroke. Sword met Scales, the two clanging in death knells, the impact hard enough to make Lisa's bones vibrate.

But she was still alive.

She heard one of the horses shriek with rage and pain. Fearing for Midnight, Lisa glanced to the right. And then War's boot slammed into her, knocking her off balance and turning her belly to mush.

Lisa tumbled to the ground, her breath knocked out of her, her stomach throbbing. God, it hurt—even worse than when she'd woken up feeling as if there were a knife in her guts. She lay there stunned for a moment, just trying to breathe and to ride out the pain, thinking, *Ow, ow, ow, ow, ow.*

Then her eyes widened as War loomed over her, Sword raised high.

"Mouse-ka-bob!" War shouted happily. Her weapon speared down.

Roll! Famine cried.

Lisa rolled. The Sword caught her coat, which let go with a meaty rip.

Get space between you, Famine told her. *Back up.*

Panting, Lisa scrambled to her feet, clutching the Scales to her chest as she backed away. Her black gaze was locked on War, who was yanking her weapon free from the muddy ground.

The mud, Lisa thought. Mud was just waterlogged soil. And she had an intimate understanding of water.

Remembering the feeling of pulling water out of the rice plants, Lisa reached out with the Scales, focusing through the symbol of Famine, shaping her desire: *push* more water into the already wet soil. Power rolled out of her in an electric wave, sizzling as it touched the ground beneath the Red Rider.

"You missed," War chortled.

Lisa said, "Wait for it."

The mud beneath War's armored boots loosened. The female knight sank down in the wet ground until she was in mud up to her shins—and even then the ground pulled at her, hungry.

"Trickery!" War struggled to free first one foot, then the other. But as soon as she pulled free, the weight of her armor dragged her back down. Her ankles pinned, War bellowed in wordless rage.

Sweating from effort, Lisa concentrated on the mud, and War was pulled down until her thighs were covered.

Lisa was swaying on her feet now, and her head was pounding. She was lightheaded, dizzy. Her strength ebbed, and her stomach was a bundle of agony. Sweating, she knew she couldn't keep this up. And as soon as she stopped, War would break free and kill her. There had to be another way.

Finish it, Famine said.

Working on it! Gritting her teeth, Lisa tried to pull War down farther, but she was too weak, and her power slipped. She grabbed hold again, but it was too late; the ground beneath the knight began to harden.

"I'll kill you," War roared, her sword slicing at the clumping mud. "I won't rest until your head is mounted on a spike! You'll die for this offense!"

Finish it, Famine said again.

How? Lisa was drenched in sweat, her limbs trembling. What could she possibly do, besides stand here and count the seconds before she died? She was as weak as when she'd been willingly starving herself.

She needed food.

War let out a victorious laugh as she pulled one leg free.

Finish it!

Food.

Tucking the Scales into the crook of her arm, Lisa dove forward and grabbed on to War's sword arm. The knight bucked and kicked, trying to shake her off like a flea, but Lisa held on fast.

And she let Famine feast.

"No," War screamed as Famine ate away at her, "you can't!"

"Yeah," Lisa answered. "I can."

War screeched, renewing her thrashing with desperate force. But the Black Rider had her now, had gotten under her skin, and her blood lust was slowly sucked away. The knight staggered, crashing to her knees. Within her armor, she began to shrivel. She doubled over until the fiery plume at the crest of her helmet touched the ground.

Lisa still held on tight, her black eyes glittering with hunger.

"You're nothing," War whispered, her voice a dying wheeze. "Nothing without me."

"Oh, shut up," Famine said, and then she sucked out War's life.

The helmet slipped off and rolled on the hardening ground. It came to a halt, its metal crusted with mud, its bloody plume sodden and limp. Empty armor fell to the ground in a clatter of plate mail and mesh, formless. The Sword slipped out of War's vacant gauntlet and landed point-first in the still-hardening mud. By the time Lisa released her power, the Sword was half buried in the road, its hilt waiting for a new master to hold it tight.

War was gone.

Lisa sat down hard on the ground, her gaze fixed on the weapon. The Scales slipped from her numb fingers and clanged to the ground. Lisa didn't notice; she was queasy—probably from overeating, ugh—and a little heartsick. Yeah, War had been about to kill her. Still, she'd utterly destroyed the Red Rider—there wasn't even a body left to bury. Her head throbbed. Lisa propped her elbows on her knees and held her head in her hands.

The Thin voice had nothing to say. Perhaps it, too, was gone. That cheered Lisa somewhat as she sat on the dusty ground, waiting for her head to clear. Belatedly, she realized the horses had stopped fighting.

And that someone was standing behind her.

"Well now," Death said, "I didn't see that one coming."

CHAPTER 17

Lisa was too tired to be afraid. Without turning around, she said, "So you're here to kill me?"

Behind her, Death let out a chuckle. It was as warm as War's had been full of malice. "Kill you? What makes you think I want to kill you?"

"Oh, I don't know. Your being death and all . . ."

A pause, and then Death asked, "Do you *want* me to kill you?"

"Not particularly, no."

"Well then, let's take that off the table, shall we?"

She glanced over her shoulder to look at him. He was still heroin-chic with long blond hair hanging in his face, his too-lazy-to-shave scruff, his long and lean physique that even his baggy, striped sweater couldn't disguise. His hands were stuffed into the pockets of his jeans, and his sneakered feet were crossed at the ankles as he leaned against his pale horse. Even with his casual pose, there was an air of menace that wafted around him like deadly cologne. The other two horses, Lisa noted peripherally, were standing opposite Death and his steed, red and black heads down in what she took to be equine bows.

Huh. Was she supposed to bow also?

"Only if the mood strikes you," Death said with a lazy smile.

Oh, right. "It's sort of unfair that you can read minds."

"Try not to think so loudly."

She decided he was joking. "If you're not here to kill me," she said slowly, "why are you here?"

He motioned to the empty armor on the ground.

"Oh," Lisa said, feeling very small. "Uh. I'm sorry about that."

He arched a pale eyebrow. "Why?"

She honestly didn't know how to answer that.

"Death is part of life," the Pale Rider said. "These things happen. Plus, she was going to kill you."

Maybe that was supposed to make Lisa feel better. "You said you didn't see this one coming. What did you see?"

"It's not as if I can read the future in tea leaves," he chided. "But since this is a business call and not a social one, frankly, I thought there would be a different Horseman standing now." He shrugged, as if in apology. "She did have an advantage."

"Sorry," Lisa said again.

Death shook his head. "You have to learn to stop apologizing for your own strength, and to stop cringing from your victories."

Her cheeks heated. "She, ah, told me she was your handmaiden."

This time when Death smiled, there was a hint of whimsy and sadness that crept by the corners. "She was. War and Death work well together."

Lisa looked down at her feet, feeling as if she'd just accidentally drowned his puppy.

"Pestilence and Famine work well together, too," Death added thoughtfully.

Okay, ew.

He laughed quietly. "It's all right, really. What she and I had can never be lost. It will always be there, like a book you can reread. But this particular chapter has come to a close."

The Pale Rider motioned with his hand, and in the ground, the Sword hilt shuddered.

"What . . ." Lisa swallowed, then tried again. "What are you doing?"

"My job."

The ground trembled and let out a terran sigh, and then the Sword unearthed itself. The weapon floated in the air, its blade gleaming and free of dirt and mud, and it glided over to Death. It hovered before him, pommel first, a breath away from his outstretched hand.

Death opened his mouth and neighed—not like a person pretending to neigh like a horse, but an actual neigh.

Oh wow, Lisa thought, one hand covering her mouth. *Oh wow oh wow . . .*

The pale horse snorted and trotted around its rider in a tight circle. When it returned to the place it started from, there was a limp saddlebag slung over its back. Lisa stared as Death rummaged through the sack she was quite certain hadn't been there a moment ago. As he dug about, a few items spilled out onto the ground: an iPod; an orange ballpoint pen with white writing on the side; a feather that was the orange-red of molten lava; a penny, green with age. Finally he pulled out a scarlet cloth the size of a handkerchief.

"The thing you want is always on the bottom," he murmured, "isn't it?" With a flick of his wrist he snapped the cloth open, and it unfolded into a blanket large enough to cover a twin bed. Death released the material, and it drifted in the air as if ready to tuck in a cloud.

Lisa was staring so hard that her eyes burned.

The Sword floated over to the scarlet cover and landed neatly in its center. The blanket wrapped itself around the weapon from tip to pommel, swaddling it like a baby with particularly sharp teeth.

"I have to admit," Death said, "the Scales are easier to package. This is sort of like a gunman encasing a rifle in a flowerbox. Which, I suppose, is appropriate enough."

Lisa wondered if Death was being chatty because he liked talking or because he needed to talk as he performed this task. She held her tongue. No matter how bad she felt about her part in War's demise, no matter how much she wondered if the man standing here in his grungy sweater and faded jeans was grieving, he was still Death. And he freaking terrified her.

She did her best not to think that last part too loudly.

The scarlet bundle floated toward the saddlebag. Death glanced down and saw the scattered objects on the ground. His mouth twisted into a rueful smile as he squatted to retrieve the fallen items. The wrapped Sword, meanwhile, disappeared inside the sack. From all appearances, the sack was empty.

Lisa blinked. *That's absolutely impossible.* But then, the Horsemen and their accoutrements of office seemed to operate outside the realm of physics—or metaphysics.

She glanced over at Death and was somewhat embarrassed to see him stroking the orange-red feather that had fallen from the saddlebag, a faraway look on his face. He tucked it into the saddlebag and murmured something Lisa couldn't hear. Feeling as if she'd just spied two lovers in a stolen embrace, she turned away. The red and black horses, she saw, were still bowing. The pale horse watched its brethren, its glowing red eyes impossible to read.

Staring at the pale steed, Lisa felt horribly out of place. And surprisingly homesick. She missed her father calling her Princess. She missed James holding her. She admitted that she missed Suzanne terribly, that she longed to talk to her again. She missed her stupid pink bedroom.

She even missed her mother.

Lisa asked herself if she could she take the reins of the black steed, knowing what that meant—knowing that she would forever be Famine. Could she do it, and accept the responsibility that came with it? The very notion made her head spin.

An idea flitted across her mind as she looked at the steeds, as she darted glances at Death. Lisa's thoughts chased one another like drunken hummingbirds, and her breath came in quick bursts as the idea formed fully.

Was it that simple?

As she wrestled with the possible implications, Death walked over to the pile of fallen armor. He crouched down and touched the helmet, lowering his head as if in prayer. Then he plucked the filthy plume and twirled it between his fingers. The mud and soil spun away, leaving the feather the fiery red of a dragon's breath—different from the feather that had fallen from his saddlebag, yet incredibly similar. Standing tall again, Death gazed upon the armor.

The ground beneath him trembled.

Death didn't lose his balance; on the contrary, he cocked his head and said something that sounded like soil eroding, or maybe like a leaf turning brown.

And then the earth swallowed War's armor.

Lisa was thrilled and amazed and terrified and in wonderment. She felt larger than a mountain and smaller than a flea—connected to everything and yet separate from all things. She was part of the fabric of the universe; she was a speck. In the face of the sublime, unable to give her feelings a voice, all she said was, "Wow."

"Wow indeed." Death chuckled as he added the red plume to his saddlebag. He pulled the drawstrings taut, the sound like a coffin sliding home. Finally, he turned to face Lisa. "Well now," he said. "Off to find a new War."

I can do this.

It wasn't the Thin voice, but the voice of Lisabeth Lewis, seventeen and so very afraid. But for the first time in a long time, she wouldn't let the fear stop her or control her. That didn't make the fear go away, but it did make it bearable. Sort of.

Lisa took a deep breath and said, "Wait."

And amazingly, Death waited. But then, Death was patient. He had no reason to rush.

"I figured something out," Lisa said quietly, "just before War and I fought. And I've been thinking about it now."

"Oh?"

Lisa lifted her chin and met Death's fathomless gaze. "I want to live."

A slow, knowing smile spread across his face. "Do you now?"

Softly, she replied, "Yes."

Death's eyes sparkled with mirth and secrets. "What are you telling me, Black Rider?"

In barely a whisper she answered, "That I don't want to be Famine anymore." No, that wasn't quite right. "That I'm not

Famine anymore." There, she'd said it. Stronger now: "I want to live my life."

"Are you certain?"

She nodded.

"Well then." Death motioned to the black horse. "Climb up. We'll finish this conversation at your house."

Of all the possible reactions Lisa had expected, that wasn't anywhere on the list. "At my house?"

"Sort of a schlep to get from this part of the world to your home. I figured you'd prefer to ride your steed one last time." Death grinned. "In another era, I would've made you walk."

Lisa gleeped, then scrambled to her steed.

"Lucky for you," Death said cheerfully, "I've mellowed out in my old age."

IIIIII

They landed in the garden beneath the girl's bedroom window; two Horsemen and three steeds. When Death and Famine slid off their mounts, the red horse made as if to bite the black one. Famine's steed would have defended itself, of course, but the pale horse flicked its ears back and whinnied softly, the warning all too clear.

Abashed, the warhorse ducked its head.

Death's steed swished its tail—both an insult and a dismissal. The black horse pretended not to notice.

The warhorse looked up, its eyes filled with rage. Snorting, the red steed clomped off to tear into the remaining rhododendrons, using teeth and hooves to batter the flowers into scented pulp.

Famine's steed exchanged a look with the pale horse, and both shrugged in their equine way. The black horse hoped the red would get a rider soon, and then go far, far away; it detested how the warhorse played with its food.

But then the Black Rider was saying farewell, and all thoughts of food were banished from the steed's mind.

‖‖‖‖

Lisa stroked Midnight's neck, her fingers lingering over the warm flesh. Even standing right in front of the steed, she could barely see him—it was a dark, dark night, and no star shone above. The moon, too, had hidden its face, giving the Horsemen their privacy.

"Thank you for letting me be your rider," she said softly.

The horse blinked at her, as if the notion of it allowing her to do anything was rather funny. Then it rubbed its muzzle in her hand.

"I'll miss you, too. I hope your next rider remembers to get you more pralines."

Midnight nickered in approval.

"Come on," Death said. "Let's get you inside."

He touched Lisa's shoulder. Coldness seeped into her, a bone-deep chill that made her teeth chatter and her breath frost. When he removed his hand, warmth flooded into her. And they were standing in her bedroom.

"Neat," she said, rubbing her arms. "If you can travel like that, why do you need a horse?"

"Company perk."

"Ah." She nibbled her lip, unsure of what to say. Her bedroom felt very small now that she had seen different parts of the world, not to mention having Death standing there like that, looking bemused. "Uh, do I have to hand in a resignation letter?"

"You have to sign your name in blood, bequeathing your firstborn son to me."

"I . . . what?"

"Kidding." Death chuckled. "Like I want to change diapers. Even one such as I has limits."

Lisa blinked. "You have a very odd sense of humor."

"Gallows humor," he said, winking. "All you have to do is return to me that which you took."

Her brow crinkled. "You mean the Scales?"

Death tapped his nose and pointed at her. "Got it in one."

Lisa's eyes widened, and her stomach dropped down to her toes. "Oh, crap! I left them back . . . back . . . back wherever it was we came from!"

"No, you didn't."

"I did, I dropped them and—"

"No," Death said, "you didn't. Well, yes, you did. But that doesn't matter, now, does it?" He made a waggling motion with his fingers.

She bit her lip, feeling incredibly stupid. *Duh.* Maybe she was quitting, but for now she was still Famine. And that meant the Scales would come when summoned. Remembering how the Scales felt in her hand, she reached out and thought, *Come to me.*

With a small pop of displaced air, the metallic balance appeared, hovering for a moment before it dropped into her outstretched palm.

Part of her wanted to close her fingers around it and go back outside to Midnight, climb on her steed's back to travel to exotic lands she'd never seen before nor even dreamed of, and taste the foods of the world. But that was only a small part of her.

And besides, Lisa was used to denying herself what she really wanted.

Swallowing the lump in her throat, she offered the Scales to Death.

He said, "Would you mind putting the Scales back in their box?"

And there on her bed was the same plain package she'd accepted from Death just the other night—a lifetime ago. "Did you wear a robe when you first came here?" she asked, carefully placing the Scales into the box.

"People see me in different ways. Sometimes I have a robe and sickle. Sometimes I'm wearing a delivery uniform. And sometimes," he said, "I can pass as a deceased rock legend."

As she tucked the lid closed, she asked, "What do you really look like, when there's no one watching?"

"If no one's watching, who's to say I have a form at all?"

Lisa smiled. If Pestilence was the philanthropist of the Horsemen, Death was the philosopher.

Once the Scales were wrapped in the package, Lisa once again offered Famine's symbol of office to Death. "I have to admit," she said, "this didn't turn out as I'd expected."

"Things rarely do," Death replied. "That's the fun thing about life. It's full of surprises. Doth thou forsake the touch of the Black Horseman?"

"Uh." The switch to Ye Olde Speake momentarily threw her, but Lisa recovered quickly. "Yes. Yes, I do."

Death took the box from her. As it left her fingers, her outfit shifted into her familiar baggy sweater and jeans. Boots misted into thick white socks. The hat disappeared, leaving her hair sloppy and windblown.

"It is done," Death said. He tucked the package into the crook of his elbow. "Thou art Famine no longer, yo. Rock on."

Lisa felt oddly hollow, as if she'd just lost a piece of herself.

"Get some rest," Death suggested. "It's been a long night. I'll see you another time."

"Oh?" She couldn't quite hide the fear in her voice.

He favored her with another of those warm smiles. "No worries," Death said, his eyes twinkling. "Unless you do something rash, it won't be for a while. Go thee out unto the world, Lisabeth Lewis. Live your life."

And then Death walked out into the moonless night.

||||||

Once she was in her pajamas, Lisa just wanted to go to bed. She was physically exhausted and emotionally drained, and the idea of sleeping for a long, long time was incredibly appealing. But as she thought about nestling under her blanket, she ran her tongue over her teeth and was dismayed to feel a fuzzy film.

She walked into the bathroom, intending to do a quick tooth brushing. But after her teeth were polished and flossed and her breath was fresh, she had to relieve herself. She lowered her pajama bottoms and her panties, and she squatted over the toilet lid. She did her business, blotted, and flushed.

And then she took off her pajama bottoms and her panties. She took off her pajama top. Naked, she stood before the full-length mirror on the bathroom door.

And as she saw how fat she was, she started to cry.

What did you think? the Thin voice asked. *That it would all just go away? That you'd suddenly not be fat anymore?*

Yes. That was exactly what she'd thought.

That's something out of a fairy tale, the Thin voice whispered. *No matter what your father thinks, you're no princess. You're just a pathetic little girl who's wretchedly fat. And no matter what you do, you always will be fat.*

Sobbing, she positioned the bathroom scale just so, and then she stepped on it for judgment.

And she was found guilty.

Numb, she put on her panties and her pajama top and her pajama bottom. She returned the scale to its proper resting place. She turned off the bathroom light and walked back to her bedroom.

The glass of water was still on her nightstand, resting on its coaster.

The pills were still in her drawer.

You don't have the guts, the Thin voice scoffed.

Through her tears, she scooped the antidepressants she'd stolen from her mother's pill case onto the nightstand. She sat on her bed. She put one pill on her tongue and took a sip of tepid water. She took a second pill, put it on her tongue, and took a second sip of water. She took a third pill, took another sip.

And she paused.

I told you, the Thin voice sneered. *You're too weak.*

But beyond the Thin voice, she heard a small, still voice tell her this: *Find the balance.*

Biting her lip, she set the glass down with a trembling hand.

The Thin voice screamed at her as she walked down the hall to her parents' bedroom. She knocked on the door.

From inside, she heard her father's voice. "Whuzzat . . . Lisa?"

"Daddy?" she called out softly. "Daddy, can I come in?"

A light peeked beneath the door. "Yes, of course . . ."

She entered, a little wobbly, her tongue too thick. Her father was sitting up in bed. Her mother's side was empty—she was away, of course, at some charity thing or another. A mostly empty glass rested on his nightstand.

"Princess," he said, alarmed, "what's wrong?"

She wanted to have him hold her and tell her all the demons were pretend, that there was no monster in her closet, that everything would be okay. But that was a lie. The demon was in her head, telling her she was too fat. She had to get the demon out. But she couldn't do it by herself.

"Daddy," Lisa whispered, "I need help."

CHAPTER 18

When Lisa opened the door to her house forty-six days later, James and Suzanne nearly bowled her over as they shouted, "Welcome home!" Lisa, standing in the doorway, looked at them both and started to laugh and cry all at the same time and then said, "I'm home again."

"We are, too, Princess," her father said with a laugh, "and we're carrying your bags, so could you please let us in?"

"Whoops." Lisa slipped to the side. Her father toted in two suitcases and her mother brought in two large boxes. One of them contained Lisa's artwork and writing journals from her time at the eating disorders facility. When Lisa had mentioned them hesitantly on the seven-hour drive home, her mom had stunned her by not only expressing interest but by asking detailed questions about what Lisa liked to write about, and did she do any poetry, and would it be okay if Lisa showed them her work once she was settled back home.

Lisa, humbled and thrilled, had said sure, she'd really like that.

Then James was scooping her off her feet, hugging her and spinning her around the room, and Lisa stopped thinking about her mother's interest in her writing. And now James was kissing her—wow, she had seriously missed his kisses—and he would've done more than that, except her folks were right there.

Ah, right.

She untangled her lips from his but kept hugging him and hugging him. He was going easy on her until she whispered in his ear, "I won't break." Then he was squeezing her for all he was worth, saying, "I missed you so much" and "I'm so glad you're back" and "Lisa" and "Lisa" and "Oh, Lisa."

She loved how her name sounded coming from his mouth.

Then Suzanne pried her out of James's embrace and hugged her just as tightly (albeit without the tongue-teasing kiss), telling her, "Leese, it's so good to see you!"

The five of them sat in the Lewis living room, Lisa on the sofa with James and Suzanne, and her parents on the love seat. They told her the same things: she looked healthy; she looked happy; and they were so thrilled she was home again. And she told them about some of the things she had learned about herself, and about the horseback riding she did at the facility, and about how wonderful the staff and the other girls in the program were.

Suzanne and James told her all about the school stuff she'd missed, the work (groan) and the gossip (whoa). Her parents told her about her great-aunt Lois's latest surgery (hip replacement) and her cousin Andy's wedding reception (a band, not a DJ).

And then the truly hard part began: they sat down at the table for dinner. Lisa was in her usual seat, with her dad at the head and her mom opposite her. James was next to her and Suzanne was across from him.

Lisa didn't realize she was sweating until James leaned over to ask if she was all right.

"Nervous," she admitted, laughing a little and feeling as if she were going to throw up.

"We're here for you," her mom said, reaching over to pat her hand. "No matter what."

"Amen," Suzanne said.

They all lifted their water glasses and toasted to Lisa's continued health and to her being home again. Clink clink, drink drink. Water wasn't a problem; there were no calories in water.

Lisa blew out a breath. No, she wasn't going to think about calories. She wasn't.

"It's okay," her dad said, smiling as he passed around the salad bowl.

Lisa took a small serving of mixed greens and passed the bowl to James. She eyed the low-fat ranch dressing and before she could overthink it, she took the bottle and squeezed a dollop onto her plate; a token amount, really, but the action mattered. She forked a bite and lifted it to her mouth.

And she paused, staring at the lettuce dipped in dressing. She tried not to think about fat and calories and how long she'd have to be on the exercise bike to work it off.

"You can do it," James said, squeezing her hand.

"I can," she said, wanting desperately to believe.

She could.

Lisabeth Lewis, seventeen and no longer Famine, took the first bite of the rest of her life.

There really was a Lisa. Different name, though. Different everything, really.

For a short time, Lisa and I had been very good friends. She was like a sister to me. She was funny and charming and smart. And one summer, she told me about her eating disorder. Lisa was bulimic. And soon, I was too.

For me, bulimia was short lived. It was the better part of one year. All the while I was binging and purging (self-induced vomiting for me; I never did laxatives or overexercised), I knew what I was doing was bad for me, but I did it anyway. I even saw a therapist. I didn't tell her I was bulimic; I told her other things, though. And at the end of the session, she said to me, "I really don't know why you're here." I never went back; I figured that if she couldn't see there was something wrong with me, she wasn't worth my time.

I don't remember when I decided my relationship with bulimia had to stop—maybe it was when my dad almost caught me vomiting upstairs. But the day came when I approached my folks and told them flat out that I was bulimic, and I knew it was bad, and I was stopping. I told them all my tricks so they'd know if I was going back to bad habits. I got lucky. I was able to stop.

Since then, the only time I've purged was when a boyfriend broke up with me a few years later. I ate a carton of ice cream, then made myself puke. (The boyfriend is just a memory now, as is the bulimia.)

Lisa and I got into a huge fight. We stopped being friends.

She's dead now. I found out about her death many years later, and it felt as if I'd been kicked in the gut.

I regret a lot of things. I regret how I didn't give Lisa a second chance when she reached out to me, years after our huge fight, asking if we could be friends again. I regret falling into dangerous habits with her in the first place. I regret the damage I did to myself, physically and emotionally.

But I don't regret our friendship.

The Lisabeth in *Hunger* isn't the Lisa from my life. But I'd like to think that Lisa's spirit would be tickled over having a book in which she—however loosely—is the heroine.

I miss you, Lisa. And I'm sorry.

||||||

There have been other stories in which an anorexic person became Famine. One of them I wrote years ago—a short story, also called "Hunger," published by the online magazine *Byzarium*. (It was a very different story than this book, but it certainly hit on some similar themes.) Another was from Marvel Comics. (Yes, I am a comic-book geek. Excelsior!) In *X-Factor,* an anorexic girl named Autumn—a mutant with the power to destroy food—was tapped by a bad guy to become Famine (not *the* Famine—no black horse for her). She and three other horsemen rode their mechanical steeds and wore bright costumes and wreaked havoc. Kapow! The good guys stopped them, of course.

I'd forgotten about Autumn, but I'm sure the notion of an anorexic teen becoming Famine started right there, when I was reading comic books. So thank you, Marvel Comics, for the spark. And thanks also to my dad, who got me into reading comic books in the first place.

Eating disorders aren't glamorous. Yes, there are a boatload of thin (and too thin) celebrities out there, on magazine covers, on television, in movies. That doesn't change anything. Eating disorders ruin lives. And they sure aren't something people can just turn on and off. Eating disorders are a disease.

Eating disorders suck.

If you have an eating disorder—whether you starve yourself or you make yourself purge or you exercise until you can't walk or you eat and eat and eat—know this: you are not alone.

And you can get help.

The National Eating Disorders Association (www. nationaleatingdisorders.org) is a nonprofit organization. NEDA provides support, both to those suffering with eating disorders and their families. NEDA helps teach people about prevention and cures. And NEDA can help people find quality care. You can call NEDA toll free and confidentially at 1-800-931-2237.

A portion of the proceeds from *Hunger* will be donated to NEDA. So if you bought this book, thank you for helping others.

ACKNOWLEDGMENTS

So many people had a hand in bringing *Hunger* to life, and I am grateful to all of them.

Many thanks to Julie Tibbott, my phenomenal editor, who believed in this book from the start, and to the entire Houghton Mifflin Harcourt team. A huge thanks to my amazing critique partner, Heather Brewer, who is just as wild about Death as I am (and I have the statue to prove it!), and to Renee Barr, who has read everything I've ever written (poor thing!). To the Mopey Teenage Bears and to the Deadline Dames—rock on! To my loving husband, Brett Kessler, for more than I could ever put into words. And to my astounding agent, Miriam Kriss, for telling me to get off my duff and write this book already—Miriam is the reason I finally got this book out of my head and onto paper, and I can never thank her enough.

During my famine research, I learned a lot about certain causes of world hunger, including rats swarming when bamboo flowers, flooded fields, and war. I learned about dirt cookies, and how some people are forced to eat the very rats that have infested their crops. I wish I could say I made all of that up.

But like eating disorders, world hunger is all too real.